Also published in Large Print
from G.K. Hall by Erle Stanley
Gardner:

The Case of the Moth-Eaten Mink
The Case of the Hesitant Hostess
The Case of the One-Eyed Witness
The Case of the Terrified Typist
The Adventures of Paul Pry, Volume 1
The Adventures of Paul Pry, Volume 2

The Case of the Sleepwalker's Niece

Erle Stanley Gardner

G·K·Hall&Co.
Boston, Massachusetts
1993

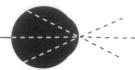

**This Large Print Book carries the
Seal of Approval of N.A.V.H.**

Published in Large Print by arrangement with
William Morrow and Company, Inc.

G.K. Hall Large Print Book Series.

Printed on acid free paper in the United States of America.

Set in 16 pt. Plantin.

Library of Congress Cataloging-in-Publication Data

Gardner, Erle Stanley, 1889–1970.
    The case of the sleepwalker's niece / Erle Stanley
Gardner.
        p.   cm. — (G.K. Hall large print book series)
  (Nightingale series)
     ISBN 0-8161-5633-6 (lg. print)
     1. Large type books.   I. Title.
  [PS3513.A6322S54 1993]
813′ .52—dc20   92-30142

Cast of Characters

in the order of their appearence

—I———————————————

PERRY MASON PACED paced back and forth across his office, thumbs hooked through the armholes of his vest, forehead puckered into a frown. "You said two o'clock, Jackson?" he asked his law clerk.

"Yes, sir, and I told her to be prompt."

Mason consulted his wristwatch. "Fifteen minutes late," he said irritably.

Della Street, his secretary, looking up from the page of a ledger, asked, "Why not refuse to see her?"

Mason said, "Because I *want* to see her. A lawyer has to wade through a lot of uninteresting murders to get something exciting. This case is a natural. I want it."

"Can murder *ever* be uninteresting?" Jackson asked.

"After you have had so many of them," Mason said. "Dead men are always uninteresting. It's the live ones who count."

Della Street, watching Mason with so-

1

licitous eyes, observed, "This isn't a murder case—yet."

"It's just as fascinating," Mason said. "I don't like being called in after the facts have crystallized. I like to deal with motives and hatreds. Murder's the supreme culmination of hatred, just as marriage is the supreme culmination of love. And after all, hatred's more powerful than love."

"More interesting?" she asked, regarding him quizzically.

Without answering, he resumed pacing the floor. "Of course," he observed, in the mechanical monotone of one thinking aloud, "the thing to do is to prevent the murder, if that's what's in the wind, but my legal training can't help appreciating what a wonderful case it would be if a sleepwalker actually killed a man, knowing nothing about it. There'd be no malice, no premeditation."

"But," Jackson pointed out, "you'd have to convince a jury that your client wasn't putting on an act."

"Couldn't the niece do that?" Mason inquired, pausing to plant his feet far apart and stare belligerently at his clerk. "Can't she testify her uncle walked in his sleep, picked up a carving knife and took it to bed with him?"

"That's what she could *testify*," the clerk said.

"Well, what more do you want?"

"Her testimony might not convince a jury."

"Why not? What's wrong with her?"

"She's peculiar."

"Pretty?"

"Yes, she has a stunning figure. Believe me, she dresses to show it."

"How old?"

"Not over twenty-three or twenty-four."

"Spoiled?"

"I'd say so."

Mason flung out his hand in a dramatic gesture. "If a pretty, twenty-three-year-old girl with a swell figure can't cross her knees in the witness box and convince a jury her uncle's a sleepwalker, I'll quit trial work." Mason shrugged his shoulders as though dismissing the subject, turned to Della Street and said, "What else is in the office, Della?"

"A Mr. Johnson wanted you to handle the Fletcher murder case."

He shook his head. "Absolutely nothing doing. That was a cold-blooded murder. Fletcher has no defense."

"Mr. Johnson says there's a chance you can plead the unwritten law, emotional insanity, and . . ."

"To hell with it. Suppose his wife *did* play around with the dead man. Fletcher's been quite a playboy himself. I've run across him in night clubs with red-hot mammas on his arm, half a dozen times in the last year. This breaking-up-a-home business is a good cause for divorce and a damned poor excuse for murder. Anything else?"

"Yes, a Myrna Duchene wants you to do something with a man who became engaged to her and skipped out with all of her savings. She now finds it's a racket with him. He's a super-sheik who makes a specialty of swindling women."

"How much?" Mason asked.

"Five thousand dollars."

"She should see the district attorney, not me," Mason remarked.

"The district attorney would prosecute him," Della Street pointed out, "but that wouldn't get Miss Duchene her money back. She thought *you* might be able to shake him down."

"Thought you said he'd skipped out."

"He did, but she's found where he is.

4

He's going under the name of George Pritchard, registered at the Palace Hotel, and . . ."

"She a local girl?" Mason interrupted.

"No. She came here from Reno, Nevada. She followed him here."

Mason squinted his eyes thoughtfully and said, "Tell you what, Della, I won't take any money from Miss Duchene, because there's only one thing for her to do, and she can do that a lot better than a lawyer can. You can give her the advice with my compliments: If this is a racket with him he'll use the coin he got from her to make a play for bigger stakes with some rich woman. He'll sink that five grand in clothes and atmosphere. Tell her to keep watch on him, and about the time he's sinking his hooks in some wealthy woman, show up and shake him down hard."

"Won't that be blackmail?" Della Street asked.

"Sure it'll be blackmail."

"Suppose they arrest her for it."

"Then," Mason said, "I'll defend her and it won't cost her a damn cent. My God, what's the world coming to if a woman can't pull a little justifiable blackmail when she's victimized! You tell her . . ."

The phone rang. Della Street said, "Hello," as she picked up the receiver, then cupped her hand over the mouthpiece and said to Mason, "She's in the outer office."

"Tell her to wait," Mason said, "I'll keep her waiting five minutes for discipline's sake. . . . No, damned if I do. I want to talk with her. Send her in. You stay, Della. Jackson, you can work on that reply brief in the traction company case."

Della Street said in an icy voice, "Tell Miss Hammer she's eighteen minutes late for her appointment but she may come in."

Jackson, tucking a pad of yellow foolscap under his arm, quietly left the office. A moment later the door from the entrance office admitted a blonde young woman in a knit sport outfit which showed the contours of her figure almost as plainly as though it had been a swimming suit. She smiled at Perry Mason, and said, so rapidly that the words almost ran together, "Oh, I'm *so* sorry I was late." She glanced from the lawyer to Della Street. Her lips remained smiling, but her eyes ceased to smile.

"My secretary, Miss Street," Perry Mason said. "Don't look like that. It won't do you any good. She stays, and takes notes. You needn't worry. She knows how to keep her mouth shut. Sit down. You wanted to see me about your uncle, didn't you?"

She laughed. "You quite take my breath away, Mr. Mason."

"I don't want to. You'll need it to talk with. Sit down and start in."

She tilted her head slightly to one side, half closed her eyes in arch appraisal, and said, "You're a Leo."

"Leo?"

"Yes, born sometime between July 24 and August 24; that's under the sign of Leo. It's a fiery, executive, magnetic sign. You're ruled by the sun. You have a robust constitution. You glory in danger, but you're susceptible to . . ."

"Forget it," Mason interrupted. "Don't waste my time telling me about my defects. You'd be here all afternoon."

"But they're not defects. It's a splendid sign. You're . . ."

Mason dropped into a swivel chair, said, "Your name's Edna Hammer? How old are you?"

"Twenty—twenty-three."

"Does that mean twenty-three or twenty-five?"

7

She frowned and said, "It means twenty-four, if you're going to be accurate."

"All right. I'm going to be accurate. You wanted to see me about your uncle?"

"Yes."

"What's his name?"

"Peter B. Kent."

"How old is he?"

"Fifty-six."

"You're living in the house with him?"

"Yes."

"Your parents are dead?"

"Yes. He was my mother's brother."

"How long have you been living in the same house?"

"About three years."

"And you're worried about your uncle?"

"About his sleepwalking, yes."

Mason picked a cigarette from the case on his desk, tapped the end on his thumbnail, raised his eyes to Edna Hammer. "Want one?" he asked, and, as she shook her head, Mason scraped a match on the under side of the desk, and said, "Tell me about your uncle."

"I don't know just where to begin."

"Begin at the beginning. When did he first start sleepwalking?"

"A little over a year ago."

"Where?"

"In Chicago."

"What happened?"

She squirmed in the chair and said, "You're rushing me off my feet. I'd prefer to tell it my own way."

"Go ahead."

She smoothed her knitted dress across her knees and said, "Uncle Pete is generous, but eccentric."

"Go on," Mason said; "that's not telling me anything."

"I'm trying to tell you about his wife."

"He's married?"

"Yes. To a hell-cat."

"Living with him?"

"No. She was getting a divorce. Only now she's changed her mind."

"What do you mean?"

"She's living in Santa Barbara. She sued for a divorce after the first sleepwalking. She claimed Uncle Pete was trying to kill her. Now she's going to have the divorce set aside."

"How?"

"I don't know; she's clever. She's an alimony hound."

"Apparently you don't like her."

"I hate her! I hate the ground she walks on!"

"How do you know she's an alimony hound?"

"Her record proves it. She married a man named Sully and bled him white. When he couldn't keep up the alimony payments and his business overhead, she threatened to have him thrown in jail. That alarmed his creditors. The bank called his loans."

"Do you mean," Mason asked, "she deliberately killed the goose that was laying her golden eggs?"

"It wasn't deliberate. You know how some women are. They think it's a crime for a man to quit loving them and that the law should inflict punishment."

"What happened after Sully went broke?"

"He killed himself. Then she married Uncle Peter, and sued *him* for divorce."

"Alimony?"

"Fifteen hundred a month."

"Your uncle's wealthy?"

"Yes."

"How long did she and your uncle live together?"

"Less than a year."

10

"And a judge awarded her fifteen hundred a month?" Mason asked.

"Yes. You see, she knows how to go about it. She puts on a swell act, and it's easy for a judge to be generous with a husband's money."

"What's her first name?"

"Doris."

"Did your uncle really try to kill her?"

"Certainly not. He was sleepwalking. He went to the sideboard and got a carving knife. She rushed back to the bedroom, locked the door, and telephoned for the police. The police found Uncle Peter standing in his nightshirt in front of the bedroom, fumbling with the doorknob, a big carving knife in his hand."

Mason made gentle drumming noises with his fingertips on the edge of his desk. "So," Mason said thoughtfully, "if it ever comes to a show-down, it would appear your uncle had tried to murder his wife, that she'd locked the door and called the police, and he'd claimed he'd been walking in his sleep, but the judge hadn't believed him."

Edna Hammer tilted her chin upward and said defiantly, "Well, what of it?"

"Nothing," Mason said. "What happened after this sleepwalking episode?"

"Uncle Pete's doctor advised a complete change, so Uncle just left his business in the hands of his partner and came back here to California where he'd always maintained his legal residence."

"And kept up his sleepwalking?"

"Yes. I was worried about him and kept watch, particularly on moonlight nights. You see, sleepwalking is connected with moonlight. Sleepwalkers become more active during the full moon."

"You've been reading up on it?" Mason asked.

"Yes."

"What have you been reading?"

"A book by Dr. Sadger, called, *Sleepwalking and Moonwalking.* He's a German. I read a translation."

"When?"

"I have the book. I read it frequently."

Mason said, "I take it your uncle doesn't know he's been sleepwalking again?"

"That's right. You see, I locked his door, but he got out somehow. I sneaked into his room the next morning to make certain he was all right. I saw the knife handle sticking out from under the pillow. I grabbed it and didn't say anything to him."

"The door was unlocked when you went in?"

"Why, yes. I hadn't stopped to think of it before, but it must have been, because I walked right in. I knew he was in the shower."

"Go on from there," Mason said.

"Uncle's coming in to see you."

Mason said, "You fixed that up?"

"Yes. At first I wanted you to put him under treatment without his knowing anything about it. Then today at lunch I fixed things so he'd consult you. He's coming in sometime this afternoon. You see, he wants to get married and . . ."

"Wants to get married!" Mason exclaimed.

"Yes, to a nurse named Lucille Mays. I like her. She understands nervous temperaments."

"How old is she?"

"Thirty-four or -five."

"How do you know she won't be another alimony hound?"

"Because she won't marry Uncle Pete until after she's signed an agreement waiving all claim to alimony and lawyers' fees, as well as all her right to inherit his property. She says if he wants to make a will

13

leaving her something, he can do that, and he can give her what money he wants her to have, but that's all."

Mason said slowly, "That agreement might be against public policy if it's that broad. They can make a marriage settlement before, and a property settlement after, the marriage. Suppose she'd feel the same way after the ceremony?"

"Sure she would. You can depend on her. She's grand. She has a little money of her own, enough to keep her, and she says if anything happens and she and Uncle Pete bust up she'll step back into her present position."

"Well, why doesn't your uncle marry her then? . . . And, if she's that kind of a woman, and he knows a good thing when he sees it, he'll give her all the breaks."

She smiled and said, "Uncle's going to settle some property on her as soon as the agreements are signed. He's letting her think she's signing away her rights, but it's only a gesture he's letting her make."

"What's holding him up? Why doesn't he marry her?"

"Well," she said, twisting uneasily under his stare, "Doris won't let them."

"Why not?"

14

"She's going to make a lot of trouble. You see, the divorce isn't final yet and she's going to claim Uncle Pete lied to her about the extent of his property and a lot of other stuff. And then she's going to claim he's insane and has homicidal tendencies and that he'll kill someone if he isn't placed in a sanitarium. You see, what she wants is to be appointed the custodian of his property."

"And that's what's worrying your uncle now?"

"That's part of it. He has other troubles. He can tell you about those. What I want you to promise me is that you'll see that he gets medical attention and . . ."

The telephone rang insistently. Della Street picked up the receiver, listened, cupped her hand over the transmitter and said, "He's in the office now."

"You mean the uncle?"

"Yes. Peter B. Kent."

Edna Hammer jumped to her feet. "He mustn't know I've been here. If you ever meet me again pretend we've never met."

"Sit down," Mason told her. "Your uncle can wait. You can . . ."

"No, no! He *won't* wait. You don't know him. You'll see."

15

"Wait a minute," Mason said. "Is there anyone in the house your uncle might want to murder?"

Her eyes were desperate. "Yes, I guess so. . . . Oh, I don't know! Don't ask me!"

She started on a run for the door. Della Street glanced up from the telephone. "Mr. Kent," she announced calmly, "has pushed his way past the girl at the switchboard and is on his way in."

Edna Hammer slammed the corridor door behind her. The door of the reception room burst open to disclose a tall, thin man. A protesting young woman held on to his coattails and half screamed, "You can't go in. You can't go in. You can't go in!"

Mason silenced her with a gesture. "It's all right, Miss Smith," he said. "Let Mr. Kent come in."

The young woman released her grasp. The tall man strode across the office, nodded to Mason, ignored Della Street, and dropped into a chair.

PETER KENT, SPEAKING in quick, nervous accents, said, "Sorry I busted in here. I can't help it; I'm nervous, I can't wait. When I want anything I want it. I'm willing to pay for any damage I did. I got a hunch to come to you. Got it while I was having lunch with my niece. She's an astrologer. She knows my horoscope by heart. She can tell me all about my planets—and I don't believe a damn word of it."

"You don't?"

"No, of course not. But I can't get the damn stuff out of my mind. You know how it is yourself. Perhaps you're walking along a sidewalk and see a ladder. If you don't walk under it, you hate yourself for being a coward. If you do, you start wondering if it'll really bring you bad luck. It gets on your nerves. You keep thinking about it."

Mason grinned, and said, "Walking under ladders doesn't bother me. I'm in hot water all the time."

"Well," Kent rushed on, "when my niece said my horoscope showed I should consult some attorney whose last name had five letters in it, I told her it was all bosh and nonsense. Then, damned if I didn't start thinking over the names of lawyers that had five letters in them. She looked up some more planets and said the name should stand for something that had to do with rocks, and did I know an attorney by the name of S-T-O-N-E. I didn't. Then your name popped into my mind. I told Edna and she got all excited, said you were the one. All bosh and nonsense! And here I am."

Mason glanced at his secretary. "What are your troubles?" he asked.

"My wife's getting a divorce in Santa Barbara. Now she's going to back up, dismiss the divorce case and claim I'm crazy.

"How far has she gone with the divorce case?"

"She's had an interlocutory decree entered."

"Under the law of this state," Mason said, "after an interlocutory decree's once entered the case can't be dismissed."

"That shows you don't know Doris," Kent said, twisting long fingers nervously as he talked. "Legislators cater to the women voters. Doris gets by because of those laws. Marriage is a racket with her, and she knows all the tricks. There's some new law that a court can't grant a final decree where the parties have become reconciled. Doris is going to file an affidavit we've become reconciled."

"Have you?"

"No, but she claims we have. She wrote me a mushy letter. I tried to be polite in answering it. She's using that as evidence. What's more, she's going to claim a lot of stuff about fraud. I don't know just what. You see, she sued for divorce mainly over some stuff which happened in Chicago, but with a few more things which happened after we got to California thrown in for good measure."

"She sued in California?"

"Yes, in Santa Barbara."

"How long had she been living there?"

"When I came from Chicago," Kent said, "I had two pieces of California property—one of them the Hollywood place, where I'm living now, and the other the Santa Barbara place. She lived with me for a few days in the Hollywood place, then went to Santa Barbara and sued for divorce."

"How about residence?" Mason asked. "Where was your legal residence?"

"In the Santa Barbara place. I had extensive business interests in Chicago and spent part of my time there, but I voted and kept my legal residence in California. Doris sued for divorce, claimed she didn't have any money, in spite of the fact she had the plunder of a couple of previous marriages salted away. She got the court to allow her temporary alimony and attorney's fees. Then she got a divorce and got permanent alimony. She's been collecting fifteen hundred dollars a month and playing around. Now she's heard I want to get married again, and she figures I'll pay a lot of money to get my freedom."

"What else?" Mason asked casually.

"I'm in love."

Mason said, "Paying fifteen hundred bucks every thirty days should be good medicine for that."

Kent said nothing. "Any other troubles?" Mason asked, as a doctor might ask for additional symptoms.

"Lots of them. My partner, for one.

"Who's he?"

"Frank B. Maddox."

"What about him."

"We're in partnership—a business in Chicago. I had to leave very suddenly."

"Why?"

"Private reasons. My health for one thing. I wanted a change."

"What about your partner?"

Kent was suddenly seized with a fit of twitching. His facial muscles jerked. His hands and legs shook. He raised his shaking hand to his twitching face, took a deep breath, then steadied himself and said, "I'm all right, just a nervous twitching that I get when I'm excited."

Mason said, watching him with eyes that were hard and unwavering in their scrutiny, "You were telling me about your partner."

Kent controlled himself by an effort and said, "Yes."

"What about him?"

"I found Frank B. Maddox, a crack-brained inventor, virtually penniless, in a little woodshed shop in the back of a rickety house in one of the cheapest districts in Chicago. He had a valve-grinding tool that he claimed could be sold to garages. He didn't even have a patent on it. The only model he had was one which had been made by hand at a prohibitive cost. I backed him and organized the Maddox Manufacturing Company in which I was a silent partner. Business was showing a fine profit when my doctor told me to quit. I left everything in Maddox's hands and came out here. From time to time, Maddox sent me accounts of what the business was doing. His letters have always been cordial. Then he wrote he had something he wanted to talk over with me and asked if he could come out for a conference. I told him to come ahead. He came out and brought a chap with him by the name of Duncan. At first he said Duncan was a friend. Now it turns out he's a lawyer, a pot-bellied, bushy-browed old fogey. He claims Maddox is entitled to draw back salary out of partnership earnings, that I wrote some letter to the owner of a patent on another valve-grinding machine saying our claims wouldn't interfere with theirs and that this letter detracted from the value of the partnership patent, which is worth a million dollars."

"In other words," Mason said, "your partner wants the business now that it's grown profitable; is that right?"

"Not only wants the business," Kent exclaimed, "but wants to bleed me for a settlement. It's the damnedest thing I ever heard of! And what makes me doubly mad is the fact that this treacherous snake came out here under the guise of paying me a friendly visit. After all I've done for him, too!" Kent jumped up from his chair, started furiously pacing the office, "Don't ever wish for money," he said; "it ruins your faith in human nature. People attach themselves like barnacles fastening to a ship's hull. You don't dare accept anyone at face value. You distrust everyone, and distrust breeds distrust."

"Specifically," Mason interrupted, "What is it you want me to do?"

Kent came striding toward the desk. "I'm going to dump my troubles right in your lap. You come out to my house, get rid of Maddox and this pot-bellied lawyer of his, then go to Santa Barbara and buy my wife off."

"When do you want to get married?" Mason asked.

"As soon as I can."

"How far shall I go with your wife?"

"Pay her seventy-five thousand dollars in cash."

"In addition to alimony of fifteen hundred a month?"

"No, that'll cover everything."

"Suppose she won't take it?"

"Then fight. . . . She's going to claim I'm crazy."

"What makes you think so?"

"When I left Chicago I was walking in my sleep."

"That doesn't mean you're crazy."

"I picked up a butcher knife and tried to get into her bedroom."

"How long ago was that?"

"Over a year."

"You're cured now?" Mason asked.

"Yes, all except for this confounded twitching and spells of nervousness."

"When do you want me at your house?"

"Tonight at eight o'clock. Bring a good doctor with you, so he can say I'm not crazy. My niece says the stars indicate this would be a good move."

Mason nodded his head slowly. "Your niece," he said, "seems to have a great deal of influence—with the stars."

"She just interprets them. She's very clever."

"Have you any other relatives?" Mason asked.

"Yes, my half-brother, Philip Rease, lives with me. Incidentally, I want him to have virtually all of my property."

"How about your niece?" Mason asked.

"My niece won't need it. The chap she's going to marry has plenty of money for both of them. In fact, it was his idea that I should make a new will. You see, Edna's just a little bit spoiled. Harris, the chap she's marrying, got the idea he'd stand more chance of having a happy marriage if he controlled the purse strings."

"Suppose she and Harris shouldn't get along?" Mason inquired.

"Then I could change my will again."

"It might be too late," the lawyer suggested.

Kent frowned, then said, "Oh, I see what you mean. I've thought some about that, too. Can't we make a will leaving my property in trust?"

"Yes, we can do that," Mason said.

"That's what we'll do, then. I want Helen Warrington, my secretary, to have twenty-five thousand dollars. She's been loyal to me and I don't want her to have to work after I'm gone. Then we can create a trust, and the income will all be paid to my half-brother so long as Edna's married to Gerald Harris. In case of a divorce, she'll share in the income."

"Does your half-brother know you're going to leave your property to him?"

"Yes."

"Suppose he'll be disappointed if you change it into a trust?" Mason asked.

"Oh, no, I wouldn't leave him anything except income," Kent said hastily. "He's not very good at investments."

"Why? Does he drink?"

"Oh, no, not that. He's a bit peculiar."

"You mean mentally?"

"Well, he's a nervous type, always very much concerned about his health. A doctor told me he was what they called a hypochondriac."

"Did he ever have money of his own?" Mason inquired.

Kent nodded, and said, "Yes, he had some rather unfortunate financial experiences, and he's become very bitter—something of a radical, you know. He was unfortunate with his own investments and he's inclined to resent any success other people have had."

"He doesn't resent yours, does he?" Mason asked smilingly.

"Very much," Kent told him.

"Notwithstanding he's to benefit by your will?"

"You don't know him," Kent said, smiling. "He's rather a peculiar temperament."

Mason toyed with a lead pencil, stared thoughtfully at Kent and said, "How about your future wife?"

"She isn't going to get a cent," Kent said. "I want you to draw up an agreement to that effect, one for her to sign before she marries me and one for her to sign afterwards. That's the only way I can be certain she isn't marrying me for my money. Incidentally, it's her idea. She says she won't marry me until I arrange things so she can't get a cent of my property, either by way of alimony or by inheritance if I die."

Mason raised his eyebrows, and Kent laughed and said, "Confidentially, Counselor, just between you and me, *after* she signs the agreements by which she can't get any money from me legally, I'm going to give her a very substantial cash settlement."

"I see," Mason remarked. "Now, about this trust arrangement providing that Edna will have an independent income in the event she divorces Harris. It may accomplish just the result Harris wished to avoid."

"I see your point," Kent said, "I guess I'll have to talk it over again with Harris. Frankly, Edna's been a problem. She was hounded to death by fortune hunters, but

I chased them out as fast as they showed up. Then Harris came along. He told me where he stood right at the start. . . . You'll meet him tonight. You let the matter of the will go for a few days, Counselor, but draw up those property agreements for my future wife and bring them to me tonight. In other words, that's something of a test. If she's willing to waive all of her rights to inherit my property then I'll *know* she's marrying me for love."

"I see," Mason said.

"Can you have those agreements with you tonight?"

"I think so."

Kent whipped a checkbook from his pocket, scribbled a check with the quick nervousness which characterized him, tore it from the book, said, "Better blot it. That's a retainer." Without another word, he turned and strode out of the office.

Perry Mason said to Della Street, with a grimace, "That's what I get for trying to be ethical and prevent a murder—a divorce case, which I don't like; a conference with a pettifogging lawyer, which is a routine I despise, and an agreement of property settlement, which is a damned chore!"

His secretary, stretching forth a coolly

capable hand, picked up the check and said, "I can see a five thousand dollar retainer, which doesn't grown on bushes."

Mason grinned and said, "Well, one thing about Kent, he's a gentleman of discernment. Bank that check before I change my mind and tell him to get another lawyer. Get Dr. Kelton on the line, send Jackson in, and ring Paul Drake at the Drake Detective Agency and tell him I have a job for him."

"You're going to use a detective?" she asked.

"On Mrs. Doris Sully Kent," he said, "and in a big way. When it comes to negotiating alimony settlements with matrimonial racketeers an ounce of information is worth a pound of conversation."

Della Street pulled a list of telephone numbers to her, moving with that unhurried efficiency which accomplishes things. Perry Mason strode to the window, stood staring meditatively down into the street below. Suddenly he turned, jerked open a drawer of his desk, and pulled out binoculars. He raised the window with his left hand, held the binoculars to his eyes, and leaned far out over the sill.

Della Street calmly hung up the receiver

in the middle of her conversation to hold a pencil poised over her notebook. Mason, eyes glued to the binoculars, called out, "9-R-8-3-9-7." Della Street's pencil wrote the number on her notebook. Mason lowered the binoculars, closed the window. "Get it, Della?"

"Yes. What is it?"

"The license number of a green Cadillac with the top down, driven by a woman in a blue dress, and trailing our client, Peter B. Kent. I couldn't see her face, but if her legs don't lie, she's got a swell figure."

——III——

PERRY MASON WAS talking with Dr. Kelton on the telephone when Paul Drake opened the door of his office and said, "Della told me to come on in, you were waiting for me."

Mason nodded, motioned him to a chair and said into the telephone, "What do you know about sleepwalking, Jim? . . . Well, I've got a case for you. The man doesn't know he's sleepwalking. He's very nervous. Carries a knife and pad-pads around the house in his bare feet. . . . You're going out with me tonight and investigate. We don't have to eat there, which is a blessing. How the hell do I know if he's going to stick a knife into us? Wear a chain-mail nightgown if you want to. I'll call for you at seven-thirty. . . . You're supposed to be checking up on him because his wife is going to claim he's crazy. . . . Well, wives do get that way once in a while. . . . Sure there's a fee it, but don't get mercenary until after you've seen the niece. . . . I'll say! . . . Okay, I'll pick you up at the club. . . ." Mason dropped the receiver back on the hook and grinned across at Paul Drake.

The lanky detective slid into the over-stuffed black leather chair and sat cross-wise, knees elevated over one arm, the other arm supporting the small of his back. "Sleepwalking, eh?" he asked, in a slow drawl.

Mason nodded and said, "Do you walk in your sleep, Paul?"

"Hell, no! You keep me so busy I don't get any sleep. What do you want this time?"

"I want some good men to look up a Mrs. Doris Sully Kent, living somewhere in Santa Barbara. Don't shadow her just yet, because she's smart and I don't want to tip my hand, but find out all about her past, her friends, finances, morals, dissipations, residence and future plans. Also get the dope on a Frank B. Maddox, of Chicago, inventor and manufacturer. He's here in the city at present, so don't bother about anything except the Chicago angle. Find out who owns a green Cadillac, license number 9R8397."

"When do you want all this?"

"As soon as I can get it."

Drake consulted his watch, said, "Okay. Do I keep the Santa Barbara investigation under cover?"

"Yes. Don't let her or her friends know she's being investigated."

Drake yawned, pulled his tall figure from the chair. "On my way," he said as he started for the door.

Della Street, hearing the door slam, entered the office.

"Where's Jackson?" Mason asked.

She smiled and said, "Packing his bag, getting ready to go to Santa Barbara and find out the exact status of the case of Doris Kent versus Peter Kent. I took the liberty of reading your mind, and giving him the order. I've telephoned the garage to fill his car with gas, oil and water and deliver it here."

Mason grinned and said, "Good girl. Some day I'll decide to raise your salary and find you've read my mind and already done it. Telephone the county clerk at Santa Barbara. Arrange with some deputy to stay after hours. Tell Jackson to telephone me and let me know what he finds out." Mason consulted his wristwatch, said meditatively, "It's about one hundred miles. Jackson should be there in something less than three hours. Tell him to step on it."

—IV—

SOMEWHERE IN THE house a clock chimed the hour of nine. Duncan was talking. For more than fifteen minutes he had been "outlining the position of his client." Maddox, a stoop-shouldered man with high cheek bones and a trick of keeping his eyes focussed on the tips of his shoes, sat silent. Kent impatiently twisted his long fingers. On his right, Helen Warrington, his secretary, sat with poised pencil. As the clock ceased chiming the hour, Duncan paused. Mason said to the secretary, "What's the last paragraph, Miss Warrington?"

Looking down at her notebook, she read, ". . . And, Whereas, the parties hereto desire, once and for all, to settle and adjust the affairs of the said co-partnership and each to release the other from any and all claims of any sort, nature, or description which he may have arising from any cause whatsoever . . ."

"That's just the point I'm making," Duncan interrupted doggedly. "My client should only release any claim he may have as a co-partner. That release covers *all* claims. The sole purpose of this compromise is to settle the partnership business. Now my client . . ."

Mason interrupted impatiently, "What claim does your client have against Peter Kent that *isn't* a partnership claim?"

"I don't know of any," Duncan admitted.

"Then it won't hurt to give a general release."

"If," Duncan countered suspiciously, "he hasn't any claim, why should it be necessary to make such a release?"

"Because I'm going to get this thing cleaned up for keeps," Mason said. "If your client does have any other claim against Kent let him make it now."

"Don't answer! Don't answer!" Duncan

exclaimed, turning to Maddox. "Let *me* do the talking."

Mason sighed. Duncan pulled a handkerchief from his breast pocket, removed his bifocals and polished them. Mason, taking a letter from a file which lay on the table in front of Kent, said, "Here's a letter signed by Maddox. Certainly you're not going back on your own client's signature. In this letter he claims . . ."

Duncan hastily took the letter, tilted his head back to peer through the lower half of the lenses, held the letter at arm's length, read it, reluctantly returned it, and said, "That letter was written before Mr. Maddox was aware of his legal rights."

Mason got to his feet. "All right," he said. "I don't like the way this business is developing. Your client either signs a blanket release or he doesn't get one damn cent. If you want to quibble him out of a good settlement go ahead."

Maddox raised his eyes from his shoe tips, flickered a brief glance at Duncan, started to say something, checked himself, remained staring steadily at his lawyer. Duncan's face flushed with anger; but he caught the meaning of Maddox's stare, said, "If you'll excuse us for a minute, I'll confer with my client."

35

He pushed back his chair. The pair left the room. Dr. Kelton, sitting a few feet back from the table, where he could study Kent's features, took a cigar from his mouth long enough to say, "You lawyers!"

Mason said irritably, "It serves me right for getting mixed up in a wrangle over a damned contract. My specialty is murder cases. Why the devil didn't I have sense enough to stick with them?"

Kent suddenly began to twitch, the twitching, starting at the corners of his mouth, spread to his eyes. He raised his hand to his face to control the twitching and the hand began to shake. Then his whole body was seized with a tremor. Dr. Kelton's eyes narrowed to watchful slits as he observed the shaking figure. By a visible effort, Kent controlled himself. The trembling ceased. He took a handkerchief from his pocket and wiped his forehead. "Don't pay him a cent," he said, "Unless you get the release we want. He's a crook. He's just a greedy . . ."

The door opened. The butler, standing on the threshold, said, "Mr. Mason on the telephone, please."

Mason strode from the room, followed the butler down a corridor to a soundproof telephone closet, picked up the receiver, said, "Well?" and heard Della Street's voice saying, "Paul Drake's in the office with a report from Chicago. Jackson's just coming on the line from Santa Barbara. Stay on after you talk with Paul and I'll give you Jackson."

Mason said, "Okay," heard the click of a switch and Paul Drake's voice saying, "Hello, Perry. I got some dope at the Chicago end of the case. Frank B. Maddox is in hot water back there. He organized the Maddox Manufacturing Company. Apparently the capital came from a Peter B. Kent. The business was built up from nothing to a tidy little industry. Kent kept in the background. Maddox did the managing. About two months ago a suit was filed against Maddox by the widow of a James K. Fogg who claims her husband invented the valve-grinding machine which is the sole product of the Maddox Manufacturing Company. It's a long story. I'll only give you the highlights. Fogg was dying of tuberculosis. Maddox posed as a friend who could do something with the invention. He took Fogg's working model and then obtained patents to it in his own name, assigned the patents to the Maddox Manufacturing Company and never accounted to Fogg for any of the proceeds. Fogg died. He hadn't been living with his wife for several months, prior to his death; but, after his death, she was rummaging through some old papers and found enough stuff to put her on the right track. She investigated and then filed suit. Maddox has been stalling the suit along. She got an order to take his deposition and has been trying to locate him to serve a subpoena, but she can't find him. The detective agency I hired to get the dope on Maddox in Chicago is also retained by Mrs. Fogg's lawyers to locate Maddox and serve the subpoena."

"Did you," Mason asked, "tell them where Maddox was?"

"No, but I want to. Can I?"

"You're damned right," Mason said gleefully. "Give them the whole story. They can arrange to serve Maddox and take the deposition here, and the sooner they do it, the better I'll like it."

"Okay," Drake drawled. "And here's something else. Your green Cadillac is the property of Doris Sully Kent of Santa Barbara."

Della Street's voice, cutting in on the

wire, said, "Just a moment, Chief. I have Jackson on the line. I'm going to switch him over to you."

Jackson's voice, quavering with excitement, said, "I've run into a mare's-nest up here."

"What is it?"

"I find that the interlocutory decree of divorce was entered exactly one year ago, on the thirteenth of the month. Hudson, Reynolds & Hunt were attorneys for Mrs. Kent. Hudson was in charge of the case. Mrs. Kent fired him this morning. She's got some attorney there in Los Angeles to represent her."

"That interlocutory was entered on the thirteenth?" Mason asked.

"Yes."

"You're certain of that?"

"Absolutely. I've checked the records."

Mason said, "Did you find out where Mrs. Kent's living?"

"Yes. It's 1325a Cabrillo Street."

Mason said, "Okay, Jackson. Here's what I want you to do. Park your car where you can watch Mrs. Kent's house. Keep the place under observation until I send someone to relieve you. She's driving a green Cadillac. Follow her if she goes out, and get the license numbers of any cars that call there. I'll have someone relieve you shortly after midnight."

Mason hung up the receiver and strode back to the library. Duncan, suspicious eyes peering out from under bushy eyebrows, was nervously twisting his cigar in his mouth. "I think," he said, "that the matter can be arranged. My client feels that Mr. Kent, probably through ignorance, disposed of some very valuable partnership assets without consulting my client; that the patents are worth . . ."

"Forget it," Mason interrupted, "you've said that at least five different times since this conference started."

Duncan raised his head to peer irritably through the lower part of his glasses at Mason. "I don't like the tone of your voice, and I don't like your comment," he said. Mason grinned at him and said nothing. "My client desires an additional ten thousand if he's to make a blanket release," Duncan said grimly.

Kent started to say something but Mason silenced him with a gesture. "I'll have to discuss this with my client," he said to Duncan.

"Very well, do you wish me to withdraw?"

"We can't reach an immediate decision. I'll want to talk things over. We'll meet tomorrow night at the same hour."

"But I thought we were all ready to conclude the matter amicably," Duncan protested. Mason said nothing. After a moment Duncan remarked, "Well, if that's final, I presume I have no other alternative but to wait."

"That," Mason told him, "is final."

Duncan turned with slow dignity, paused in the doorway only long enough to say good night in a voice which failed to conceal his disappointment, then, ushering his client into the hallway, slammed the door behind him.

Kent said, "Dammit, Mason, I wanted to settle. Money doesn't mean much to me, but as you know, I want to get my affairs in order . . ."

"All right," Mason interrupted. "Now *I'll* tell *you* something: Maddox is a crook. Tomorrow we're going to file suit against Maddox alleging that he defrauded you by claiming he was the owner and inventor of the Maddox Valve grinding Machine, whereas he wasn't the owner, wasn't the inventor and had obtained the working model by defrauding a man by the name of Fogg who was the real inventor. You're going to demand an accounting, have a receiver appointed for the business in Chicago and you're going to throw Maddox and Duncan out on their ears."

"You mean Frank didn't invent that machine?"

"Exactly. He stole the whole business."

"Why, dammit, I'll have him arrested! I'll fix him! I'll go to him right now and . . ."

"Forget it," Mason broke in. "You've got more important stuff to think of. Mrs. Fogg's suing Maddox in Chicago and trying to reach him with a subpoena. He's out here trying to shake you down for what he can get, grab the cash and skip out. If you tip your hand now, Mrs. Fogg will never be able to take his deposition. You're going to stall him along and keep him here in the house until the subpoena can be served on him in the Fogg case. But you've got other things to think of. Your former wife canned her Santa Barbara lawyers and hired someone here in Los Angeles. It's going to take a little time for this Los Angeles lawyer to get started. An interlocutory decree was entered in the Santa Barbara divorce case a year ago today. Tomorrow morning I can walk into court—if I walk in ahead of her lawyers—and get a final decree of divorce. As soon as I get it, you can legally marry."

"But doesn't that take three days' notice?"

"In this state, but not in Arizona. I'm going to have you sign the necessary affidavit to get a final decree. The court will grant it as a matter of course. You and Miss Mays fly to Yuma and wait until I telephone you that the final divorce has been granted. Then go ahead and remarry. That marriage will be legal."

"Does it have to be done that quickly? Couldn't we wait to give Miss Mays a chance to get packed, and . . ."

"Can't you see," Mason exclaimed, "the minute the former Mrs. Kent files those papers, you *can't* get married until the litigation's disposed of. But if you can beat her to it, get a final decree and remarry, you'll be in an impregnable position."

Kent jumped to his feet, started for the door. "Come on, Helen," he said. "You'll have to get the plane reservations." Together, they left the room.

Mason turned to Dr. Kelton. "Well, Jim, what do you think of him?"

Dr. Kelton puffed meditatively on his cigar, took it from his mouth, and said, "Perry, I'll be damned if I know. That act he put on was a fake."

"You mean that shaking business?"

"Yes."

"Then that isn't a symptom of some nervous disorder?"

"No. Certain involuntary repeated contractions of associated muscles constitute a malady generally known as *Tic*. Excluding a form of trigeminal neuralgia due to degenerative changes in the nerve, *tics* aren't painful. But this isn't a *tic*. Watching him closely, I'd be willing to swear he's faking."

"But why," the lawyer asked, "should Kent want to fake a nervous disorder? He's fighting his wife's claim that he is deranged. *He's* trying to show that he's perfectly sane. That's why he had me bring you out here."

Dr. Kelton shook his head. "He's the one that suggested you bring a doctor to observe him?"

"Yes. I think that his niece had something to do with the suggestion, but it came from him."

"He had you bring me out here," Dr. Kelton said slowly, "so that he could put on that act in front of me. Like most laymen, he exaggerated his ability to fool a doctor. He might have been able to fool a family physician into making a wrong diagnosis, but that shaking business wouldn't fool a psychiatrist."

"Then what's he building up to?" Mason asked. Kelton shrugged his shoulders. "How about the sleepwalking? Does that indicate anything?"

"You mean as a symptom of mental derangement?"

"Yes."

"No, sleepwalking is usually due to some emotional inhibition, an arbitrary association of ideas with the individual. It isn't a sign of mental derangement. It comes nearer being a species of individual hypnosis, an auto-suggestion of the subconscious."

"Do sleepwalkers become more active at the full of the moon?"

"Yes."

"Why?"

"Frankly, Perry, we don't know."

"Well," Mason said, grinning, "this is a new one—a client retains me to prove he's sane and then tries to act goofy."

Dr. Kelton took the cigar from his mouth

and said dryly, "Not to mention his amiable habit of prowling around the house at night carrying a carving knife."

—V———

LUCILLE MAYS, LONG-LIMBED, lean-waisted, tall, met Perry Mason's appraising eyes with frank candor. "I'm a nurse," she said. "Mr. Kent is twenty years older than I am. Naturally, people think I'm marrying him for his money. I'm not. I just wanted to give you my personal assurance I'd sign anything which would protect Mr. Kent."

Mason nodded. "Thanks," he said. "I'm glad to have had the chance for this talk. By the way, have you ever talked this over with Mr. Rease?"

She laughed and said, "No. Mr. Rease doesn't like me. He's a hypochondriac and he doesn't like people who won't humor him. Harris, that's Edna's wealthy fiancé, humors him all the time. Why, just tonight Rease complained his room was draughty and Harris humored him and fixed things up so he'll change rooms with Maddox. Mr. Kent won't like it when he finds it out. I've repeatedly explained to him he mustn't give in to Rease's imaginary ailments."

"Kent doesn't know about it?" Mason asked.

"No. It was right after dinner. Peter was telephoning. The others were all there, and . . ."

The door opened. Kent bustled into the room, slipped his arm protectingly about Lucille Mays' waist. "If we go into the solarium," he said, "we'll be just in time for a drink. Harris is mixing one of his famous cocktails."

Lucille Mays nodded, but her eyes remained fixed on Mason's. "Very well," she said, "I just wanted you to know where I stand, Mr. Mason."

Mason nodded, said to Kent, "I want to prepare an affidavit for your signature so we can get that final decree. Also, I want to send someone to Santa Barbara to relieve my man up there. He's keeping watch on Doris Kent."

Peter Kent motioned toward a door which led to an adjoining room, from which came sounds of laughter. "I want you to meet my niece," he said, "and Jerry Harris is here. He's the young man she's engaged to. He'll be willing to do anything he can to help out."

Mason nodded, permitted himself to be escorted through the door into a room, one end of which was devoted to a bar. Behind the bar, a grinning young giant in shirt sleeves was shaking cocktails. Edna Hammer stood with one foot on the brass rail, saying, "Does this look about right?" At the other corner of the bar, Helen Warrington, Peter Kent's secretary, was toying with the stem of a cocktail glass, her eyes showing good-natured amusement.

"No," the man behind the bar was saying, "you don't look drunk enough. If we're going to put on this act and . . ." He broke off as his eyes caught sight of Perry Mason.

Kent said, "I want to present Perry Mason, the lawyer—my niece, Miss Edna Hammer, and Jerry Harris. You've met Miss Warrington. I believe that Jerry is about to mix one of his famous K-D-D-O cocktails."

Edna Hammer came from the bar to give Perry Mason her hand. "I've heard so much about you," she exclaimed. "It's a real pleasure. Uncle told me he was going to consult

48

you, and I've been hoping I'd have a chance to meet you."

Mason said, "Had I known your uncle had such a beautiful niece I'd have insisted on a drink earlier in the evening."

"Well put," Harris exclaimed, "and just for that I'm going to initiate you to the famous Harris K-D-D-O cocktail."

"Just what," Mason inquired, "is the K-D-D-O cocktail?"

It was Helen Warrington who answered. "The letters," she said, "stand for knock-down-and-drag-out."

Kent walked to the end of the bar, knocked on the mahogany with his knuckles as though he had been calling a directors' meeting to order. "Folks," he said, "a serious situation has developed. Let's cut out the comedy for a minute. I want your help."

The smiles instantly faded from their faces. "I'm going to be married," Peter Kent said, "tonight—or rather, early in the morning."

Harris started to applaud, but as he caught the expression on Kent's face, dropped his hands back to his sides. "Now, then," Kent went on, "I haven't any secrets from anyone in this room. You're all my friends. I know I can depend on you. I'm going to put the cards on the table. Mr.

49

Mason wants some assistance. He wants someone to go to Santa Barbara right away."

"Count me in," Harris said, raising his hand. "Volunteer number one."

Kent nodded his thanks, and said, "Here's the situation: Doris, whom you all know, and whose character you understand without any comments from me, is planning to start lawsuits which will block my marriage. However, due to a change of lawyers, her suit has been delayed. If Mr. Mason can get a final decree of divorce at Santa Barbara tomorrow morning before the other actions are filed, Lucille and I can fly to Yuma, Arizona, and be married."

Harris reached for his coat. "If you want someone to drive you to Santa Barbara, Mr. Mason," he said, "I've got a Rolls-Royce out in front that will make the trip in less than two hours from here. It's done it before."

Mason said slowly, "I don't want to go myself. I've a clerk up there I can trust. I want to send him a good stenographer so he can prepare some pleadings if it becomes necessary. I also want someone who knows Doris Kent to keep watch on her residence and let me know if she either comes in or goes out. Then I'll arrange to have detectives called in. The person who knows her can 'put the finger on her' and the professional detectives can carry on from there."

"I know her," Harris said. "Edna introduced me to her a month ago." He turned to Edna Hammer and said, "Come on up, Edna, it would be a nice lark."

Edna Hammer hesitated, glanced at Helen Warrington; and Peter Kent, interpreting that glance, said, "Go ahead, both of you girls go up. I won't be needing Helen for anything. She's had experience as a legal stenographer, and she can be available if anything breaks."

Mason nodded brief thanks. "That's taken care of, then," he said. He went to the telephone, called his office, and said to Della Street, "Prepare an affidavit for final judgment of divorce in the Kent case. The interlocutory decree of divorce was granted in Santa Barbara a year ago, on the thirteenth. You'll have to leave the number and page of the judgment book blank until we can get the data. It was entered on the same day it was made."

"I already have that," she said calmly. "I have the affidavit all prepared and the final decree of divorce ready for the judge's signature."

"Been reading my mind again, eh?" he asked.

"You'd be surprised," she told him. "Do you come after the affidavit or do I bring it over?"

"Where's Paul Drake? Is he there?"

"No, he went out. He's been in and out all evening."

"Has he found out anything new?"

"I don't think so."

"Get a cab," Mason told her, "and come on out."

By the time Mason hung up the telephone, Helen Warrington, on an extension telephone which had been plugged into a phone jack back of the bar, had a call through to the airport. "I have a pilot who can furnish a bi-motored, cabin plane," she said, "but he wants to wait until daylight to make the trip. He says he can leave at daylight and have you in Yuma by seven-thirty in the morning."

Kent looked questioningly at Mason. The lawyer nodded his head. "That's okay," Kent said. "Charter the plane."

Abruptly he began to shake, his arms, legs and face twitching. He turned his back as though to hide his affliction. Helen Warrington said in a coolly capable voice, "Very well, have the plane ready to start at daylight."

The butler opened the door, said to Helen Warrington, "Mr. Peasley calling, Miss Warrington."

Kent abruptly snapped out of his jerking fit. "Look here," he warned, turning to face them, "not a word of this to Bob Peasley."

"Really," Helen Warrington said, "unless it's imperative that I go . . ."

"*I* want you to," Edna Hammer said petulantly. "After all, you know, it's going to be an all-night trip."

"Tell Peasley," Kent said, "that you're going out on business for me; don't tell him how long you'll be gone or where you're going. Tell him he'll have to excuse you tonight."

"And don't tell him who you're going with!" Harris laughed. "He'd stick a knife into me."

Helen Warrington said to the butler, "Show Mr. Peasley in."

"Well," Harris said, "since I'm going to drive the car, I'll keep sober, but there's no reason on earth why *you* folks can't have one of the famous Harris K-D-D-O cocktails as a stirrup cup."

"Yes," Edna Hammer said, "give Bob one. It'll do *him* good." There was a touch of acid in her tone.

The door opened. A stoop-shouldered young man of about twenty-five gave a perfunctory, generally inclusive nod, said, "Good evening, everyone," and let his eyes turn at once to Helen Warrington.

She moved to his side. "Mr. Mason, Mr. Peasley," she said.

"Perry Mason!" Peasley exclaimed. "The lawyer!"

"In person," Mason agreed, shaking hands, "and about to sample one of the famous K-D-D-O cocktails of our esteemed contemporary, Jerry Harris, admittedly the greatest bartender of the post-prohibition era."

Kent moved over to Peasley's side. "I'm sorry, Bob, but you'll have to excuse Helen this evening. She's going to be very busy."

Peasley made an attempt at a smile. "That's all right, I only dropped in for a minute, anyway. I've got a hard day ahead of me at the office tomorrow. I just wanted to talk with Helen for a moment." His eyes fastened upon Helen Warrington significantly.

"Everyone excuse us, please," she said gayly. "Save my K-D-D-O cocktail, Jerry Harris."

She nodded to Bob Peasley. They left the room, and Edna Hammer heaved a sigh of relief. "Deliver me from a jealous man!" she said. "Did you notice the way he looked at you, Jerry?"

"Did I!" Harris remarked, pouring ingredients into a cocktail shaker. "One would think I was *the* Don Juan of Hollywood."

Edna Hammer's tone was slightly wistful. "Are you, Jerry?" she asked.

"Darned if I know," he told her, grinning. "It's hard for me to keep track of *all* the competition; but I do my best."

Lucille Mays, who had been talking in a low voice with Peter Kent, suddenly laughed, and said, "I'll bet you do at that, Jerry."

"Sure," he told her, "I'm not kidding. It's the only way I can put my stuff across. You see, it's only natural for women to want the man that all other women want. Therefore, by making all women want me I make all women want me, whereas if women didn't want me, no woman would want me."

"*I* hate *me,*" Lucille Mays said, laughingly.

"No," Jerry told her, "it's a serious truth," and then, turning audaciously to Edna Hammer, he said, "Isn't it, sweetheart?"

Edna Hammer laughed up at him and said, "It is with me, Jerry, but when *I* sink my mud hooks into you, don't forget you'll be branded. If I see any woman hanging around I'll stick a knife in her."

Harris, carefully measuring the last of the cocktail ingredients into the shaker, said, "A couple more of these, sweetheart, and you'll be more liberal minded."

Edna said to Harris, "Hurry up, Jerry; Mr. Mason's being courteous and gallant, but I can see he's just seething with important thoughts. . . . *Leo's* are like that."

"Am *I* a *Leo?*" Jerry asked. "I seethe with important thoughts."

"You," she told him, her eyes suddenly filled with sombre fire, as her voice lost its bantering tone, "are a *Taurus*—and how I like it!"

PERRY MASON, CLAD in pajamas, stood at the bedroom window, looking down on the patio which was drenched with moonlight. The big house, built in the form of a "U," surrounded a flagged patio, the eastern end of which was enclosed by a thick, adobe wall some twelve feet high. Dr. Kelton, his huge bulk sagging one of the twin beds, rubbed his eyes and yawned. Mason surveyed the shrubbery which threw black shadows, the fountain which seemed to be splashing liquid gold into the warm night, the shaded alcoves, striped awnings, umbrellas and scattered garden tables. "Delightful place," he said.

Dr. Kelton yawned again and said, "I wouldn't have it as a gift. Too big, too massive. A mansion should be a mansion. A bungalow should be a bungalow. This business of building a hotel around an exaggerated patio makes the whole thing seem out of place."

"I take it," Mason remarked, turning to face Dr. Kelton, and grinning, "you didn't have a particularly pleasant evening."

"I did not, and I still don't know why the devil you didn't let me go home after I'd looked Kent over."

"You forget that you're going to get up at daylight to see the bridal party off."

Kelton's head shook in an emphatic negative. "Not me. I'm going to stay right here. I've practiced medicine long enough to value my sleep when I can get it. I don't get up any morning to see any bridal party off on any airplane."

"Don't be such a damned pessimist," Mason said. "Come take a look at this patio in the moonlight, Jim, it's beautiful."

Dr. Kelton stretched out in the bed to the tune of creaking springs. "I'll take your word for it, Perry. Personally, I don't like the place. I'll feel a damn sight easier when I get out of here."

"Worried about someone sticking a carving knife in your ribs?" Mason asked.

Dr. Kelton, sucking in another prodigious yawn, said, "For God's sake, turn out the light and come to bed. Listening to you two lawyers wrangling I got so sleepy I . . ." There was a faint scratching sound on the panels of the door. Kelton sat bolt upright, said in a low voice, "Now what?"

Mason, finger on his lips, motioned for silence. After a moment, the same scratching sound was repeated. "Sounds," Mason said, grinning, "as though someone with a carving knife were standing just outside your door, Jim." He opened the door an inch or two, and showed surprise. "You!" he exclaimed.

"Well, let me in," Edna Hammer said in a hoarse whisper.

Mason opened the door, and Edna Hammer, clad in a filmy negligee, slid surreptitiously into the room, closed the door behind her and twisted the key in the lock.

"I say," Dr. Kelton protested, "just what *is* this?"

"I thought you went to Santa Barbara," Mason remarked.

"Don't be silly. I couldn't go. Not with Uncle Pete walking in his sleep, and this the night of the full moon."

"Why didn't you say so, then?"

"Because I was in a spot. You and Uncle Pete wanted Helen Warrington to go so she could help your assistant up there. Naturally she wouldn't go unless I went. I might have explained, but Bob Peasley showed up, and if he'd thought Helen had been planning to go to Santa Barbara alone with Jerry . . . Well, he'd have killed Jerry, that's all."

"But I still don't see why you couldn't have said frankly that you didn't care to go," Mason said.

"I didn't want Uncle Pete to be suspicious. He'd have realized something was wrong."

"So what did you do?"

"So I went out to the car, explained to Jerry and Helen exactly how things were. They were very nice about it, as soon as they understood."

Dr. Kelton said, "Is that any reason why you two should put on night clothes, and hold conferences in *my* bedroom?"

She looked at him, laughed, and said, "Don't be frightened. I won't bite. I want Mr. Mason to come with me while I lock Uncle Pete's door and the sideboard drawer."

"Why can't you do it alone?" Mason asked.

"Because if anything *should* happen, I'd want you as a witness."

"I'd make a poor witness," Mason laughed. "Dr. Kelton makes a swell witness. Get up, Jim, and help the girl lock up."

Kelton said in a low voice, "You go to the devil, Perry Mason, and let me sleep."

"I haven't a robe with me," Mason said to Edna Hammer. "Do I go wandering around the house in slippers and pajamas?"

"Sure," she told him. "Everyone's in bed."

"If it's okay with you, it is with me," he told her, "let's go."

She unlocked the door, looked cautiously up and down the corridor. Moving on silent feet, her progress accompanied by the rustle of silk, she led the way to her uncle's bedroom door. Kneeling before the lock, she gently inserted a key, taking care to make no noise. Slowly, she turned the key until, with an almost inaudible click, the bolt shot home. She nodded to Mason, resumed her progress toward the stairs. Near the head of the stairs she whispered, "I oiled the lock so it works smoothly."

"Doesn't your uncle have a key?" he asked.

"Oh, yes, but he'd hardly get the keys out of his pocket and unlock the door if he were asleep. You know a sleepwalker wouldn't do that."

"How about the sideboard?"

"*I* have the *only* key for that drawer."

She produced a small flashlight, lit the way to the sideboard and inserted the key in the top drawer.

"The carving set's in there?" Mason asked.

She nodded, turned the key, clicking home the bolt.

"I'm *so* glad you came out here tonight," she said. "You're getting things fixed up. Uncle is better already. I feel certain he'll get a good sleep tonight and won't do any sleepwalking."

"Well," Mason said, "I'm going to keep *my* door locked."

She clutched at his arm and said, "Don't frighten me or I'll shock your doctor friend to death by staying all night in your room."

Mason laughed, followed her back up the stairs, paused at the door of his room, turned the knob, grinned and said, "Jim beat me to it. He locked the door after we left."

"Perhaps," she giggled, "he's afraid that *I'll* walk in *my* sleep."

Mason tapped on the panels, and after a moment, the floor creaked with the sound of a ponderous body moving in slippered feet. Then the bolt shot back and the door opened. Edna Hammer pushed Perry

Mason to one side, thrust in her head and said, "Boo!"

A half second later the bed spring on Kelton's bed gave forth violent creaks. Perry Mason followed Edna Hammer into the room. She approached the bed. "Do *you*," she asked Dr. Kelton, "walk in *your* sleep?"

"Not me," Kelton said, managing a grin, "I stay put—but I snore to beat hell, in case you're interested."

"Oh, lovely," she exclaimed. "Think of what a *swell* sleepwalker you'd make. You could walk in a fog and blow your own signals." She turned with a laugh, slid her fingertips along the sleeve of Mason's pajamas, said, "Thanks a lot. You're a big help," and sailed through the door with fluttering silks trailing behind her.

Jim Kelton heaved a sigh. "Lock that door, Perry, and for God's sake, *keep* it locked. That woman's got the prowls."

—VII—

A SMALL ALARM clock throbbed into muffled noise. Mason reached out, switched off the alarm, jumped from bed, and

63

dressed. Dr. Kelton quit snoring for a matter of seconds, then resumed his nasal cadences. Mason put out the light, opened the door and stepped into the corridor. Edna Hammer was standing within a few feet of his door. She was still attired in her negligee. The aroma of freshly made coffee filled the hallway. "What are you doing here?" he asked.

"I sneaked up to tell you I'd unlocked Uncle's door, and to ask you to smuggle me a cup of coffee."

"Can't you ring for the butler and have him bring it to your room?"

"No. I don't dare to. No one must know I didn't go to Santa Barbara. Uncle Pete would be furious if he thought I'd slipped something over on him. And then I have Helen to consider."

Mason nodded. "Which is your room?" he asked.

"In the north wing, on the ground floor next to the 'dobe wall. It opens on the patio."

"I'll do the best I can," he promised. "Your uncle's up?"

"Oh, yes, he's been up for half an hour, packing and puttering around."

A door knob rattled. Edna Hammer gave

a startled exclamation and was gone with a flutter of silken garments. Mason walked toward the stairway. Peter Kent, freshly shaved, opened a door, stepped out into the hallway, saw Mason and smiled. "Good morning, Counselor. I hope you slept well. It's splendid of you to get up to see us off."

"I always get up to see my clients married," Mason said, laughing, "but it looks as though I'm going to be the only one. Dr. Kelton's sound asleep and refuses to budge."

Peter Kent looked at his watch. "Five o'clock," he said musingly. "The sun rises about six. We're to be at the field at five forty-five. That will give us time for bacon, eggs and toast, but we'll have to make it snappy."

He accompanied Mason down the flight of stairs to the big sitting room, where the butler had a cheerful fire going in the fireplace and a table set in front of it. Lucille Mays came toward Peter Kent with outstretched hands, starry eyes. "How did you sleep?" she asked solicitously.

Kent's eyes met hers. "Wonderfully," he said, "Counselor Mason inspires confidence. I'm sorry I didn't consult him earlier."

Mason returned Lucille Mays' smile. They seated themselves at the table, had a hurried breakfast. As Kent started upstairs, Mason poured himself another cup of coffee, sugared and creamed it, strolled toward the door, ostensibly to look out into the patio.

Mason waited until they had left the room, then moved quickly down the long corridor. Edna Hammer was waiting for him, the door of her room open. Mason handed her the cup of coffee, said in a whisper, "You didn't tell me whether you liked sugar or cream, so I took a chance."

"Just so it's hot coffee," she said. "My Lord, I feel all in!"

"Cheer up," he told her. "It'll soon be over. We'll know by ten o'clock, perhaps a little before."

She took the coffee, thanked him with a smile, slipped into the room and closed the door. Mason returned to the living room. The butler, cleaning up the things, said, "Your cup and saucer, sir?"

Mason made a shrugging gesture. "Set it down somewhere," he observed, "and can't remember where. Doubtless it'll show up. I was looking at some of the paintings in the corridor and then I walked out into the patio for a while."

"Very good, sir," the butler said.

"What's your name?" Mason asked.

"Arthur—Arthur Coulter."

"You act as chauffeur as well as butler?"

"Yes, sir."

"What make of car does Mr. Kent have?"

"A Cadillac and a Ford cabriolet. I'm getting out the sedan this morning. I believe he said you were to drive it."

"That's right. You'd better get started, Arthur."

The butler vanished with the smooth, noiseless efficiency of a well-trained domestic. A moment later, Kent, carrying a suitcase and an overcoat, stood in the doorway, said, "You'd better get your coat, Mr. Mason."

"It's in the hall," Mason answered.

He went to the reception hall, found his coat and hat. Almost at once they were joined by Lucille Mays. Kent opened the door. There was the sound of a purring automobile motor. The beams of headlights crept around the curve in the driveway. A shiny Cadillac slid smoothly to a stop. Coulter climbed from the driver's seat, opened the car doors, handed in the two light bags. Mason slid in behind the wheel, laughed and said, "There should be one or two more. I feel as if I were chaperoning a honeymoon."

"You," Kent told him, "are Cupid."

"It's a new rôle," Mason said, "but I'll try to live up to it." He slid back the shifting lever, eased in the clutch and as the car purred into smooth motion, said, "Let's go over things now to be sure we have everything straight."

Kent pulled up one of the folding seats, sat in it and leaned forward so that his head was within a few inches of Mason's shoulder. "I'm to go directly to the courthouse in Yuma," he said. "Is that right?"

Mason nodded and for a few moments gave his attention to shifting gears. Then he said, without taking his eyes from the road, "Yes. Hunt up the telephone operator if they have a private switchboard, and, if they don't, find out who answers the telephone in the clerk's office. Tell them you're expecting an important call and make arrangements so it'll come through without delay. I'll telephone you as soon as the final decree has been granted. After that, you can make headquarters at the Winslow Hotel at Yuma. Wait there. If you don't hear from me again by six o'clock in the afternoon you can start on a honeymoon, but let me know where I can locate you."

"You're going to file action against Maddox?" Kent asked.

Mason's jaw squared. "I'm going to take that boy down the line," he promised, "but I think we'll file the action in Chicago. There's a matter of venue I want to look up."

"You'll let him know that there'll be no compromise?"

"You can leave Maddox to me," Mason said grimly, pushing the accelerator down almost to the floorboards.

——VIII——

PERRY MASON TAPPED gently on the door of Edna Hammer's bedroom. She opened it and said, "How did you leave the honeymooners?"

"Very much up in the air," he answered, grinning, "and I hope you don't throw me out for that one."

"Come in and tell me about it. Remember, I'm a woman, and marriage means a lot to us, so don't you omit one single detail."

Mason seated himself, grinned and said,

"We went to the airport. A pilot with a helmet dangling in one hand came forward and introduced himself. There was a cabin plane drawn up. The motors were running. Your uncle and Miss Mays entered the plane. We did a little wise-cracking back and forth. Miss Mays blew me a kiss. The pilot got in, taxied the ship down the field, turned around, tested first one motor, then the other, came back into the wind and took off. The sun was just rising. The hills back of Burbank were a beautiful blue, and . . . Oh, yes, I nearly forgot, the weather report said there was clear visibility, gentle shifting winds, unlimited ceiling and good flying conditions all the way to Yuma."

"Oh, you unromantic lawyers!" she exclaimed.

"And what did *you* do?" Mason asked.

"I was simply ravenous," she said. "As soon as you folks had left I telephoned for a taxicab to come to the corner and wait. I sneaked out the back door, took the cab into Hollywood and got myself a light breakfast. Then I came sweeping back to the house in a taxicab, and announced I'd taken a bus back from Santa Barbara and was famished. I've ordered breakfast. It's coming up in a few minutes."

"The butler," Mason said, "wondered what happened to my coffee cup. I strolled off with it and he missed it."

She frowned. "It's here in the room. I'll take it out on the patio and leave it on one of the tables. Perhaps we'd better go now." She picked up the cup and saucer from the dresser. "My, I *really* feel like a criminal. Do all lawyers make people so delightfully furtive?"

"I'm afraid you can't blame your capacity for intrigue upon your counsel . . . not after the way your stars told your uncle he should consult an attorney whose name contained five letters and stood for a stone or something similar."

She giggled delightedly and said, "I don't know *what* I'd do without my astrology. And the, funny part of it is my uncle claims he doesn't believe in it.'

"Do you believe in it?" Mason asked.

"Why not?"

The lawyer shrugged his shoulders.

Sun was peeping into the patio. Edna Hammer sat down in one of the reclining chairs, placed the cup and saucer on a coffee table, inspected it critically and said, "It doesn't look exactly right there, does it?"

"No," Mason said. "Frankly, I think your butler was just a little suspicious—not that it makes any great difference now your uncle has gone."

"Oh, but it does," she said. "I couldn't run out on Helen Warrington. You don't know Bob Peasley. My heavens, he'd tear Jerry limb from limb—that is, he'd try to." She paused to laugh at the idea of the somber Peasley becoming physically violent with the big, broad-shouldered Harris. She picked up the cup and saucer, moved a few steps to one of the tiled coffee tables and pulled a catch. The hinged top swung upward, disclosing an oblong receptacle underneath the top. "I presume it was originally designed for holding knives, forks, spoons and napkins, but it makes a fine place to ditch things," she said.

Mason watched her. Turning, she caught his eye and asked, "Why the expression?"

"What expression?"

"The peculiar look in your eye."

"I didn't know there was one."

"What were you thinking of?"

"I was just thinking how little chance a clumsy man has when it comes to dealing with the finer mind of a woman."

"In other words, that's a nice way of saying that you think I keep bamboozling my uncle?"

"It depends on what you mean by bamboozling."

"I don't see anything wrong with using such mental faculties as you have in order to get what you want, do you?" she asked.

He shook his head and added, "Particularly when those mental faculties are accompanied by beauty."

She said wistfully, "I wish I were beautiful. I'm not. I've got a swell figure, I know that. But my features aren't regular. There's too much animation in my face. I think a girl, to be beautiful, has to keep her face in repose. It makes for that virginal, doll-like something men like in their women, don't you think so?"

"I hadn't given it any particular thought —not along those lines," Mason replied.

"I've given it lots of thought. I'd like to use my beauty. That's what it's for. Lots of people think I deliberately dress to show my figure. I do. I'm proud of it. Perhaps I'm a pagan little animal. Bob Peasley says I am. But I revel in having a good-looking figure. I guess I don't know what modesty . . ."

"I think," Mason interrupted, "your but-

73

ler seems to have something on his mind. He's approaching rather purposefully."

She broke off, stared at the butler and said in swift, low tones, "Remember, he *mustn't* know I was here last night."

She faced the butler, said, "What is it, Arthur?"

"Beg pardon," he said, "but the sideboard drawer—I can't get the top drawer open. It seems to be locked."

"Oh!" she exclaimed, then, after a moment, "are you sure you looked all around for the key, Arthur?"

"Yes, ma'am."

"Did you look in the little brass bowl over to the right of the pitcher?"

"No, ma'am, I didn't look there."

"Well, let's go look. It must be around there somewhere." She gave Mason a meaning glance, started walking rapidly. Mason fell into step at her side and the butler followed, a deferential pace or two in the rear. At the sideboard, she tried the drawer, said, "It's locked all right," and then started looking around on the top of the sideboard, her hands fluttering swiftly about various places. "It must be here somewhere, Arthur," she said, in the tone of a magician handing out a line of "patter" by which the attention of an audience is kept from his hands. "The key was in the drawer yesterday, I know. Someone must have inadvertently locked the drawer and placed the key somewhere nearby. It's inconceivable that anyone would have carried it away. There can't be anything in that drawer which . . . Why, *here* it is! It was right under the fold of this throw."

The butler watched her as she fitted the key to the drawer and turned the lock. "I'm sorry that I bothered you," he said. "I couldn't find it. I thought perhaps you knew where it was."

She turned the lock, pulled the drawer open, suddenly gasped, and stood staring downward at a plush-lined receptacle for a carving set. A smooth-finished black horn-handled fork glittered in its hollowed receptacle, but the place which should have held the carving knife was empty. She glanced significantly at Perry Mason, her eyes dark with panic. Then she said, "Just what was it you wanted, Arthur?"

"I'll get it, Miss Edna, it's quite all right. I just wanted the drawer opened." He took out some salt dishes, and closed the drawer.

Edna Hammer raised her eyes to Perry Mason, then slipping her hand under his elbow, gripped his forearm and said, "Do come back out in the patio. I love it out there in the early morning."

"What time are you going to have breakfast?" Mason asked. "I think we should go up and arouse Dr. Kelton."

"Oh, we sort of single-shot on breakfast. We have it whenever we get up."

"Nevertheless," Mason said significantly, "I think Dr. Kelton would appreciate it if we called him."

"Oh, I see," she exclaimed quickly, "Yes, yes, you're quite right. Let's call Dr. Kelton."

They walked toward the stairs. She said in a low voice, "I didn't get you for a minute. You want to look in Uncle's room?"

"We might as well."

"I can't understand it. You don't suppose there's any possibility . . . that . . ."

As her voice trailed away into silence, Mason said, "You didn't look in the drawer last night before we locked it."

"N-n-n-no," she said, "I didn't, but the knife *must* have been there."

"Well," Mason said, "we'll see what we'll see."

She ran up the stairs ahead of him, her feet fairly flying up the treads, but when she had approached the door to her uncle's bedroom she hung back and said, "Somehow, I'm afraid of what we're going to find here."

"Has the room been made up yet?" Mason asked.

"No, the housekeeper won't start making beds until around nine o'clock."

Mason opened the door. She entered the bedroom a step or two behind him. Mason, looking around him, said, "Everything seems to be in order—no corpses stacked in the corners or under the bed."

"Please don't try to keep my spirits up, Mr. Mason. I've got to be brave. It's under the pillow, if it's anywhere. That's where it was the other morning. You look, I don't dare."

Mason walked to the bed, lifted the pillow. Under the pillow was a long, black-handled carving knife. The blade was discolored with sinister reddish stains.

——IX——

MASON DROPPED THE pillow, jumped backwards and clapped his hand over Edna Hammer's mouth. "Shut up," he said, stifling the screams she had been about to emit. "Use your head. Let's find out what we're up against before we spread an alarm."

"But the knife!" she half screamed as he lowered his hand from her lips. "It's all b-b-b-bloody! You can see what's h-h-h-happened. Oh, I'm so f-f-f-frightened!"

"Forget it," Mason told her. "Having hysterics isn't going to help. Let's get busy and find out where we stand. Come on."

He strode out into the corridor, walked down to the door of his room, tried it, found it locked, banged on it, and, after a moment, heard the sound of heavy steps, the clicking of a bolt, and Dr. Kelton, his face covered with lather, a shaving brush held in his right hand, said, "I'm already up, if that's what you came for. The smell of broiling bacon filters through that window and . . ."

"That," Mason told him, *"isn't* what we came for. Get the lather off your face and come in here. You don't need to put on a shirt, just come the way you are."

Dr. Kelton stared steadily at Mason for a moment, then went to the washstand, splashed water on his face, wiped off the lather with a towel, and, still drying his face and hands, accompanied them across the corridor to Peter Kent's room. Mason raised the pillow. Dr. Kelton leaned over to stare at the bloody blade, so eloquent in its silent accusation. Kelton gave a low whistle.

"It'll be Maddox," Edna Hammer said, her voice hysterical. "You know how Uncle Pete felt toward him. He went to bed last night with that thought in his mind. . . . Oh, hurry, let's go to his room at once! Perhaps he isn't dead—just wounded. If Uncle Pete was groping about in the dark . . . perhaps he . . ." She broke off with a quick, gasping intake of her breath.

Mason nodded, turned toward the door. "Lead the way," he ordered.

She led them down the corridor, down a flight of stairs, into a corridor on the opposite wing of the house. She paused in front of a door, raised her hand to knock and said, "Oh, no, I forgot Maddox changed rooms with Uncle Phil. Maddox is over here."

"Who's Uncle Phil?" Dr. Kelton asked.

"Philip Rease, Uncle Pete's half-brother. He's something of a crank. He thought there was a draught across his bed and asked Maddox to change rooms with him last night."

She moved down to another door, knocked gently, and, when there was no answer, glanced apprehensively at Perry Mason and slowly reached for the door knob. "Wait a minute," Mason said; "perhaps *I'd* better do this." He pushed her gently to one side, twisted the knob and opened the door. The room was on the north side of the corridor. French doors opened onto a cemented porch some eighteen inches above the patio. Drapes were drawn across these windows so that the morning light filtered into the room, disclosing indistinctly a motionless object lying on the bed. Mason stepped forward and said over his shoulder to Dr. Kelton, "Be careful you don't touch anything, Doctor."

Edna Hammer came forward a doubtful step or two, then walking rapidly to Perry Mason's side, clung to his arm. Mason bent over the bed. Abruptly the figure below him stirred. Mason jumped back. Frank Maddox, sitting up in bed, stared at them with wide eyes, then, as his surprise gave way to indignation, he demanded, "What the devil's the meaning of this?"

Mason said, "We came to call you for breakfast."

"You've got a crust," Maddox said, "invading the privacy of my room this way. What the devil are you trying to do? If you've been through any of my private papers, I'll have you arrested. I might have known that Kent would resort to any underhanded tactics. He poses as a big-hearted magnanimous individual, but it's all pose with him. Dig below the surface, and you'll find out just what a damn skunk he is."

Mason said in a low voice, "How about Mrs. Fogg, Maddox—is *she* a skunk, too?"

Maddox's face showed sudden dismay. After a moment he said, "So you know about *her?*"

"Yes."

"And that's what you came to see me about?"

"On the contrary," Mason said, "we came to call you for breakfast. Come on, let's go."

"Wait a minute."

Maddox thrust his feet out from under the covers, groped for his slippers. "About this Fogg business, Mason, don't believe everything you hear. There are two sides to that."

"Yes," Mason remarked, "and there are two sides to a piece of hot toast. Right now I'm interested in both of them. We'll discuss the Fogg matter later."

He led the way from the room, holding the door open until the others had stepped into the corridor, then pulling the door shut behind him with a bang. "What's the Fogg case?" Edna Hammer asked.

"An ace I was keeping up my sleeve; but when he started making a fuss I had to play it. He'll be a good dog now."

"But *what* is it?" she asked. "If it concerns Uncle Pete, I . . ."

"While we're here," Mason said, "I think we may just as well take a complete census."

"What do you mean?"

"Let's just make certain none of the others are—indisposed. Who sleeps here?"

"Mr. Duncan."

Mason pounded his knuckles on the door. A booming voice said suspiciously, "Who is it?"

Mason smiled at Dr. Kelton and said, "Notice the legal training, Jim. When I knocked at *your* door you opened it. When

I knock at a lawyer's door he wants to know who it is."

"Perhaps he's hardly presentable to ladies," Dr. Kelton pointed out, but Duncan, fully dressed, even to his necktie and scarf pin, flung open the door, saw who it was, and glowered at them in belligerent appraisal.

"Well," he asked, "what do you want?"

"First call for breakfast," Mason told him.

"Is this," Duncan asked, adjusting his spectacles, and raising his head so that he could regard them through the lower part of the bifocals, "a new innovation which Mr. Kent has instituted?"

"You may consider it such," Mason replied, turning away from the door.

"This room," he asked Edna, "is, I suppose, where your Uncle Phil sleeps." He indicated the door before which she had first paused.

"Yes. Maddox slept there until last night, then Uncle Phil changed with him."

"Well," he said, "let's call your Uncle Phil."

He tapped on the panels. There was no answer, and he tapped more loudly. Duncan, who had been standing in his doorway, came striding out into the corridor and said, "What's the big idea?"

Mason, his face showing a puzzled expression, pounded loudly with his knuckles, turned the knob, opened the door and entered the room. Mason took a single step toward the bed, whirled around, blocked the others in the doorway, and said to Dr. Kelton, "Get that girl out of here."

"What's the matter?" Edna Hammer asked, and then, as she interpreted his silence, screamed.

Duncan, pushing importantly into the room, said, "What's the trouble here? What's happening?"

Maddox, attired in pajamas and slippers, shuffled along the corridor until he joined the group in the doorway. Dr. Kelton, taking Edna Hammer by the arm and pushing her from the room, remarked to the other two, "Just keep out, please." Duncan's big paunch blocked the doorway. Dr. Kelton, also heavily fleshed, but not as big in the stomach, pushed up against Duncan. "Let the woman out," he said.

Duncan shoved. "I've got a right to know what's happening here," he said.

"Let the woman out," Dr. Kelton repeated.

Duncan cleared his throat, continued to shove. Dr. Kelton, slightly lowering his shoulder, braced himself, gave a heave, sent Duncan staggering backwards. Edna Hammer, sobbing into her handkerchief, left the room. Duncan, recovering his balance, pushed through the door, saying, "You saw what he did, Maddox. Let's get at the bottom of this."

Mason, raising his voice, called to Dr. Kelton. "I think you'd better come back, Jim, we'll want a medical man, and I want some witness to see that these two buzzards don't frame anything."

Duncan protested, "Upon behalf of my client, I resent . . . Oh, my God . . . Oh, my good God, the man's been murdered!"

Dr. Kelton, walking to the bed, looked down at the blood-stained bedclothes, at the greenish-gray features which stared with glassy eyes half open. He placed his fingers on the sides of the neck, turned to Mason and said, "It's a job for the coroner—and the police."

"We're all getting out of this room," Perry Mason ordered, raising his voice. "A murder's been committed. The Homicide Squad will want things left exactly as they are. Everybody leave the room, please, and don't touch anything."

Duncan, glowering suspiciously, said, "And that applies to you as well as to us."

"Certainly it does."

"Go ahead and get out, then, don't think you can herd me around like a sheep. I don't know what authority you have to take charge of things."

"I suggested," Mason told him, "that we'd *all* leave the room. If *you* want to stay, that's quite all right."

He pushed past the paunchy lawyer, said, "Come on, Jim, we've given them warning. If they want to stay in here, they can explain it to the Homicide Squad."

Duncan, suddenly suspicious, grabbed Maddox by the arm. "Come out, Frank," he said, "come on out. He's trying to trap us."

"They knew someone had been murdered. They thought *I* was the one," Maddox said.

"Come out, come out," Duncan insisted. "We'll talk outside. I have some information, but I'll only give it to the police. Don't let that man Mason frame anything on you, Frank." They scrambled from the room.

"I demand," Duncan said, in the corridor, "that the police be called in immediately."

Perry Mason was moving toward the telephone. "You're not demanding any louder than I am," he retorted. He reached the telephone and called police headquarters, said to the desk sergeant, "There's been a murder committed at the residence of Peter B. Kent. It's in Hollywood at 3824 Lakeview Terrace. . . . This is Perry Mason, the lawyer, talking. . . . I'll explain that when you get here. I've closed up the room. Very well, I'll lock it, if I can find the key."

As Mason turned from the telephone, Dr. Kelton drew him to one side. "There's one angle of this you want to consider, Perry."

"What's that?"

"*If,*" Dr. Kelton pointed out, "your client, Peter Kent, had intended to commit a deliberate murder, he's laid a swell foundation by building up this sleepwalking business."

"What makes you think he planned anything like that, Jim?"

"That shaking act he put on."

Mason suddenly faced Dr. Kelton. "Look here, Jim," he said, "if you don't want to miss all your morning appointments, you'd better get out of here. I'll have to stick

around. There's no reason for you to."
Dr. Kelton nodded. His face showed relief. "You can," Mason said, "take my
car."

—X————————————————

MASON GAVE EDNA HAMMER low-voiced instructions in a corner of the patio. "No
matter *what* happens," be said, "no one
must know anything about this Santa Barbara angle of the case." He looked at his
watch and went on, "We've got to hold
your Uncle Peter absolutely in the clear for
at least two hours and a half."

"You mean they'll want to bring him
back?"

"They'll want to question him."

"Will they want to bring him back?"

"Probably."

"What *will* I tell them?"

"Tell them that you don't know where
he is."

"I'm going to tell them that I spent the
night in Santa Barbara and came back on
the bus."

Mason squinted his eyes, and said, "I
wouldn't advise you to do it."

"But I'm *going* to do it."

"They'll check up on you."

"They won't have any reason to check up on me. But what will *you* tell them about Uncle Pete?"

"I," Mason said, "won't tell them a damn thing."

"Won't they make trouble for you?"

"They may try to."

"When will they question me?"

He looked at his watch again. "Almost any minute now. They're examining the room and the body. Duncan's bursting with a desire to spill some information. I don't know what it is. Probably it's something that's only about half as important as he thinks it is. Both he and Maddox hate your Uncle Pete and they hate me. We can't tell just exactly what they'll do nor how far that hatred will take them."

"They wouldn't commit perjury, would they?"

"I wouldn't put it past either one of them. Maddox is a crook. I think Duncan is a pettifogger. They were both trying to shake your uncle down. I stood in the way of that and naturally they resent it."

"But what can they do?"

"I don't know. That remains to be seen.

In the meantime I want to put in a telephone call. You hold the fort."

"Okay. But remember I came here in a taxicab after spending the night in Santa Barbara."

"Don't tell them where you spent the night," he warned. "Refuse to do that until after you've consulted me."

"Will that make trouble?" she asked.

"Plenty," he told her, "but anything you can do is going to make trouble. Tell them that where you spent the night doesn't have the faintest bearing on the murder case but does concern your uncle's business affairs. But remember this, sooner or later they're going to put you under oath and then you've got to tell the truth."

"Why?"

"Because they'll prosecute you for perjury if you don't."

"Oh, dear. . . . I'm not going to tell them anything."

"All right," he said cheerfully, "don't tell them anything."

"But you won't give me away?"

"Listen," he said, "any information that they get out of me you can put in your eye. *I'm* going to telephone." He went to the soundproof telephone closet and called

90

Della Street. "Della," he said, when he heard, her voice on the line, "something's happened out here. Get Paul Drake to pick up a couple of good men and come out. They probably won't let him in, but he can hang around and find out as much as he can. Have you heard anything from Santa Barbara?"

"Yes. Jackson telephoned just a few minutes ago. He said he and Mr. Harris took turns watching Doris Kent's house all night; and she didn't go out anywhere, but Jackson has something he wants to tell you personally. He says he doesn't want to tell it over the telephone."

"Why not?"

"IIc said that it was filled with dynamite."

"Who's watching the house now?"

"I think Mr. Harris is. Jackson said that he kept on duty until some time before midnight, when Harris relieved him, and that Harris wants to be relieved."

"Tell you what you do, Della. I think Drake's agency has a man up in Santa Barbara. Tell Paul to get some photographs of Mrs. Kent, and a good description of her. Then he can contact Harris and take over the job of watching. I want to know when she leaves the house, and if possible, where she goes. Tell Jackson to get that final decree just as quickly as he can. Tell him to keep you advised by telephone. I'll get the information from you. Have you got that straight?"

"Yes," she said. "What happened out there?"

"A carving knife got stained," he said.

There was a moment of silence during which only the sound of the buzzing wires came to his ears. Then she said, "I see."

"Good girl," Mason told her, and slipped the receiver back on the hook. He left the closet and found Edna Hammer in the hallway.

"Everything okay?" she asked. He nodded. "You're fixing things so Uncle Peter can get married?" she asked.

"I want to do the best I can for my client," he told her.

The eyes which regarded him were filled with shrewd appraisal. "You're a clever lawyer, aren't you?"

"Meaning what?" he asked.

"Meaning," she said, "that I happen to know it's the law of this state that a wife can't testify against her husband. If Uncle Pete and Lucille Mays are married, then *she* couldn't testify to anything against him, could she?"

Perry Mason raised his eyebrows. "I don't know what she *could* testify to. . . . Here comes Sergeant Holcomb now."

"Tell me," she said, grasping Perry Mason's wrist with cold fingers, "are *you* going to stand by Uncle Pete?"

"I always stand by a client."

"How far?"

"If," he said, "your Uncle Pete committed a cold-blooded, deliberate murder, I'm going to tell him to plead guilty or get some other lawyer. If he killed a man while he was sleepwalking I'm going to go the limit for him. Does that satisfy you?"

"But suppose he *did* commit a cold-blooded, deliberate murder, as you call it?"

"Then he can either plead guilty or get some other attorney to represent him."

"Who's going to decide whether he committed a coldblooded murder?"

"I am."

"But you're not going to decide hastily. You won't jump at conclusions? Promise me you won't."

"I never do," he said grinning. "Good morning, Sergeant Holcomb."

Sergeant Holcomb, who had been striding down the corridor toward them, looked from Perry Mason to Edna Hammer. His eyes were glittering with suspicion. "It looks very much," he said, "as though you're instructing this young woman what to say."

"So often appearances are deceptive, Sergeant," Perry Mason said suavely. "Miss Hammer, permit me to present Sergeant Holcomb."

The sergeant paid not the slighest attention to the introduction. "How does it happen *you're* here?" he asked Perry Mason.

"I'm negotiating an agreement between a chap by the name of Maddox, and Mr. Peter Kent."

"And where's Peter Kent?"

"I'm sure I couldn't tell you."

"Why not?"

"It would be betraying the confidence of a client."

"Bosh and nonsense!"

Mason bowed and said, "That's the way *you* feel about it, Sergeant. *I* feel that it would be betraying a professional confidence. That means, of course, it's merely another one of those differences of opinion we have so frequently."

"And after you've said that," Sergeant Holcomb said, "then what?"

"After that, I'm quite finished."

"I still don't know where Kent is."

"Doubtless," Mason said, "there are other sources of information available to you."

Holcomb swung to Edna Hammer, "You're his niece?"

"Yes."

"Where's your uncle now?"

"I'm sure I couldn't tell you."

Holcomb's face darkened with rage. "I've sent for Sam Blaine, the deputy district attorney. You two come into the living room." Sergeant Holcomb turned on his heel and strode down the long corridor toward the living room.

"You," Perry Mason told Edna Hammer, "had better tell them the truth."

"I can't."

He shrugged his shoulder, placed his hand under her elbow, walked down to the living room with her. They found the others assembled, a solemn, hushed group. Sergeant Holcomb looked at his watch, said, "Sam Blaine, the deputy district attorney, should be here any minute. I want to ask a few questions. Who's the dead man?"

Duncan, raising his voice, said, "I'm an attorney. I think I can be of some help to you in this. I have some *very* valuable information."

"Who's the dead man?" Holcomb asked.

"He's Phil Rease, a half-brother of Peter Kent," Maddox answered.

"Who are you?"

"I'm Frank B. Maddox. I'm Mr. Kent's business partner, the President of the Maddox Manufacturing Company of Chicago."

"What are you doing here?"

"Straightening out some business matters with Mr. Kent, and this is Mr. Duncan, my attorney."

"You're the one Mason was dealing with?" Holcomb asked.

"Mr. Mason," Duncan observed pompously, "represented Mr. Kent. He was here last night, and he spent the night in this house. He had a doctor with him. Dr. Kelton, I believe the name was."

Holcomb turned to Mason, asked, "Where's Kelton?"

"He had some important cases. He couldn't wait. Naturally, you can locate him at any time you desire."

Maddox volunteered a statement. "This man, Mason," he said, "Dr. Kelton, and Miss Hammer *knew* that someone had been

96

murdered. They didn't know who it was. They were prowling around looking us over this morning. They thought I was the one that had the knife stuck in me."

"How did you know someone was murdered, Mason?" Sergeant Holcomb asked,

Mason's eyes widened. "I didn't."

The door opened, and Arthur Coulter, the butler, showed a dapper young man, with eye glasses from which dangled a long, black ribbon, into the room. "Here's Sam Blaine," Sergeant Holcomb said. "He'll take charge of things."

Blaine, freshly shaven, his tan shoes glittering, his white linen gleaming, smiled inclusively, and said, "Just a minute while I get posted." He led Sergeant Holcomb off to a corner where the two conversed for several moments in low tones. When they had finished, Blaine returned, drew up a chair at the head of the table, opened his brief case, produced a notebook and said, "Did any of you hear anything suspicious during the night?"

Duncan cleared his throat importantly, "I'd like to make a statement," he said, "I think I can tell you *exactly* what happened."

"Who are you?" Blaine asked.

"John J. Duncan, a lawyer."

"Go ahead," Blaine invited.

"Shortly after midnight last night I was wakened by someone walking past the French windows. It was moonlight. The shadow fell across me. I am a very light sleeper. I think the person was barefooted."

"What did you do?"

"I had a glimpse of this person walking past my room. There's a cement porch in front of the French windows. I jumped to my feet and ran to the windows. It was full moon. I saw someone sleepwalking."

"How do you know this person was sleepwalking?" Blaine asked.

"From the manner in which the person was attired, and the peculiar walk. The figure wore a nightgown. The head was thrown back, I knew instantly it was a sleepwalker."

"Was it a man or a woman?"

"Er—Er—well, you see, it was moonlight and . . ."

"Never mind answering that question now," Blaine said hastily, "what did this person do?"

"Walked across the patio, fumbled around with one of the coffee tables for a minute and raised the lid. Then the figure disappeared through a door in the north side of the patio—a door which enters a corridor."

"You saw this?"

"Very clearly."

"How do you fix the time?"

"By the clock which was by my bed."

"What time was it?"

"Quarter after twelve o'clock. I couldn't get back to sleep for a long time."

Blaine asked Edna, "Are you Miss Edna Hammer?"

"Yes."

"What do you know about this?"

"Nothing."

"Did you see anyone enter your room last night?"

"No."

"Was your door locked or unlocked?"

"Locked. I'm nervous at night. Almost a month ago I had a new spring lock put on my bedroom door. I have the only key to it."

"Did you know someone had been murdered this morning?"

"Certainly not."

"Did you leave your room last night?"

She hesitated and said, "Where I was last

night doesn't have any bearing on the matter."

Blaine asked, "Where is Peter Kent?"

"Ask Perry Mason," Sergeant Holcomb said, "he seems to know."

Mason said, "My client, Mr. Kent, is absent on a business matter which has nothing whatever to do with the present situation."

"When did he leave?"

"I can't answer that question without betraying the confidence of a client."

"When's he coming back?"

"I think I can promise that he'll return either late tonight or early tomorrow morning."

"Where is he now? This is a serious business, Mason. Don't try to stall. We want to question your client."

Mason shrugged his shoulders and said nothing.

"Look here," Blaine threatened, "if *you* don't dig up your client now, we're going to find out where he is and *drag* him in."

"Go ahead," Mason remarked, "drag him in."

"Who knows where he is?" Blaine asked.

For a moment there was silence, then Maddox said, "I happen to know that Mr. Jerry Harris, Miss Edna Hammer, and Miss

Helen Warrington, Mr. Kent's secretary, all left last night upon a mysterious errand. I think they went to Santa Barbara. There's a chance Mr. Kent went with them."

"Santa Barbara, eh? What are they doing in Santa Barbara?" Blaine asked.

"I'm sure I couldn't tell you."

Blaine turned to Sergeant Holcomb, said in a low voice, "I don't think we're going to get anywhere this way. We'd better talk with these people one at a time and we'll want the servants as well. Will you please have everyone leave the room but remain available for questioning?"

Sergeant Holcomb nodded importantly. "The patio," he announced, "is the proper place. You folks all go out in the patio and don't start talking among yourselves. . . . Hadn't we better finish with Perry Mason and keep him away from the rest? He's representing Kent. We might find out a lot more if we get through with Mason first."

Blaine said, "Good idea. What do you know about this, Mason?"

Mason waited until the shuffling confusion of moving feet had ceased, then said, "I was negotiating an agreement, between Kent and Maddox. For certain reasons, which I won't bother to discuss at present,

101

it became advisable to postpone the negotiations. I remained here last night. I slept in a room in the upper floor with Dr. Kelton. This morning Peter Kent left on a business trip. I may say that that trip was taken at my suggestion. I have no intention of disclosing his destination. After he left, Miss Hammer called my attention to the fact that the carving knife was missing from the sideboard. I happened to know that Peter Kent had previously walked in his sleep. I believe it is a matter of record that he picked up a carving knife on that occasion."

"Where's the record?" Blaine interrupted.

"In a divorce case filed against him by his wife, Doris Sully Kent."

"Where?"

"In Santa Barbara."

"Go on. What did you do?"

"I went with Miss Hammer to Mr. Kent's bedroom. I raised the pillow on his bed and found the knife under his pillow."

"Under his pillow!" Blaine exclaimed.

Mason nodded coolly. "The knife was, and is now, under the pillow of Peter Kent's bed. I didn't touch it. But as soon as I saw it, I suspected what had happened.

Therefore, I aroused Dr. Kelton, and, in company with Miss Hammer, we made a round of the guests. We found Mr. Rease lying in bed, the covers up around his neck. Apparently he had been stabbed through the covers. I didn't make a close investigation. As soon as I found the body I left the room and telephoned police headquarters."

"Why the devil didn't you tell Sergeant Holcomb about this before?"

"He wouldn't let me. He was in examining the body. I tried to go in and he told me to stay out."

Blaine said to Sergeant Holcomb, "Send a couple of men up to look under that pillow. Don't let anyone touch that knife until we have a fingerprint man go over the handle. . . . How long have *you* been here, Sergeant?"

"About ten minutes before I telephoned you," Holcomb answered.

"And I got here in ten or fifteen minutes," Blaine said. "That makes less than half an hour. . . . What's this lawyer's name . . . oh, yes, Duncan, I'll get him and take a look at that coffee table."

Blaine walked out toward the patio. Sergeant Holcomb called two men and ran up the stairs to Kent's bedroom. Mason followed Blaine, saw him speak to Duncan. They walked toward the center of the patio. Duncan paused uncertainly, went to one of the coffee tables, shook his head, moved over to the one under which Edna Hammer had placed the coffee cup and saucer. "This the table?" Blaine asked.

"I believe it is."

"You said the top came up?"

"It seemed to. He raised what looked like the top and then let it drop back with a bang."

Blaine looked the table over and said, "There seems to be an oblong receptacle under this table top . . . Wait a minute, here's a catch."

He shot the catch and raised the top of the table.

"Nothing in here," he said, "except a cup and saucer."

"Nevertheless, this is the place," Duncan insisted.

Edna Hammer said very casually, "I'll take the cup and saucer back to the kitchen."

She reached for it, but Blaine grabbed her wrist. "Wait a minute," he said, "we'll find out little more about that cup and saucer before we take it anywhere. There may be fingerprints on it."

"But what difference does *that* make?" she asked.

The voice of the butler from the outskirts of the little group said, "Begging your pardon, sir, but I happen to recognize that cup and saucer. . . . That is, at least I recognize the saucer. You see, it has a peculiar chip out of it. I knocked that chip out this morning."

"What time this morning?"

"Shortly after five o'clock."

"What were you doing with a saucer shortly after five o'clock?"

"Serving breakfast to Mr. Kent, Miss Lucille Mays, and Mr. Mason."

"Then what did you do?"

"Then I brought up the Cadillac and Mr. Kent, Miss Mays and Mr. Mason drove off. After an hour or so, Mr. Mason returned the car."

"You don't know where they went?"

"No, sir, but I think they were going to get married."

"And what have you to say about this cup and saucer?"

"This saucer, sir, went with the cup out of which Mr. Mason was drinking his coffee. I didn't have time to replace the chipped saucer. They seemed to be in a bit of a hurry, and Mr. Kent had told me to see that breakfast was ready to serve at twenty minutes past five on the dot. He was most punctual."

"So you drank out of this saucer, Mason?" Blaine asked.

Mason shook his head and said, "Certainly not."

"You didn't?"

"No," Mason said. "I never drink out of a saucer when I'm visiting." Blaine flushed and said, "I meant, you had the cup and saucer. If you want to be technical, you drank out of the cup."

"That's what the butler says," Mason said. "Personally I wouldn't be able to tell one cup from another. I admit that I drank out of *a* cup this morning."

"Then what happened?"

"Begging your pardon, sir," the butler said, "Mr. Mason walked out with the cup and saucer. I couldn't find it afterwards and asked him what he'd done with it and he said he couldn't remember; that he thought he'd set it out in the patio some place."

"At five-twenty this morning?"

"That would have been approximately five-thirty, or five-forty."

"What was *he* doing out in the patio at five-thirty?"

The butler shrugged his shoulders.

Blaine turned to Mason, and asked, "What *were* you doing out here at five-thirty?"

"I *may* have been out here," Mason said slowly, "but I have no independent recollection of it."

"Did you put that cup and saucer under the top of the table?"

"I did not."

"Do you know who did?"

"I think," Mason said, "you're making a mountain out of a molehill. Here's a saucer with a chip out of it, and you're wasting valuable time inquiring how I happened to drink my coffee and where I was standing when I did it, when the crying need is for a solution of this murder. It isn't a question of who drank the coffee. The question is who stuck the knife . . ."

"That'll do," Blaine interrupted, "I'm thoroughly capable of carrying on this investigation." Mason shrugged his shoulders. "It may be well for you to remember," Blaine said significantly, "that, according to the testimony of this disinterested witness, Mr. Peter Kent, who apparently is your client, deposited something in this receptacle at around midnight. Now then, we find that thing is gone, and in its place a cup and saucer which, concededly, had been in your possession."

"I haven't conceded it," Mason replied. "It may or may not have been the cup and saucer I was using. As I mentioned, cups look alike to me, and Duncan didn't identify the sleepwalker as Peter Kent, either."

"It's the *saucer* that has the distinctive chip out of it," Blaine pointed out. Mason shrugged his shoulders, lit a cigarette and smiled. Blaine said, "Very well, Mr. Mason. I think we'll take your statement in front of the Grand Jury. I know you only too well. We won't get anywhere by trying to interrogate you when we haven't any power to *make* you answer questions. You're trying to stall things along. You're just leading us around in a circle."

"You mean that you're finished with me?"

"Do you know anything more about the murder?"

"Nothing.

"Yes, we're finished with you. When we

want you we know where to get you, and," he added significantly, "we know *how* to get you—*with a subpoena.*"

Mason bowed and said, "Good morning, everyone."

He caught Edna Hammer's eye and saw that she was pleading with him, trying to express some unspoken message. He moved toward her and Blaine interposed. "I said that you could be excused, Mason," he said. "I think this inquiry will progress a lot faster and a damned sight more efficiently if we examine the witnesses before they have had the benefit of your *very valuable* suggestions."

Mason smiled and bowed mockingly. "I wish you luck," he said.

—XI—

Mason found Paul Drake seated in a car parked at the curb half a block away from the Kent residence. "I tried to get in," Drake said, "but they turned me back. I've got a couple of men ready to go to work on the witnesses as soon as the cops quit keeping the place sewed up. What happened?"

"Plenty," Mason told him. "A fellow by the name of Rease was killed. He was stabbed in bed, evidently while he was asleep. The covers were up around his neck. The night was rather warm. There were only two light blankets over him. The knife was shoved down through the blankets."

"Any motive?"

Mason lowered his voice and said, "There's damn near a case of circumstantial evidence against Peter Kent. He's my client."

"Where's he now?"

"Gone bye-bye."

"You mean he's running away?"

"No, he's on a business trip."

"Are you going to surrender him, Perry?"

"It depends. I want to find out first whether he's guilty. If he is, I don't want to handle the case. *I* think he was walking in his sleep. If he was, I'm going to try to get him off."

"What kind of a man was the chap who was killed?"

"Sort of a crank. He was always worrying about his health."

"Did Kent have some particular motive for killing him?"

"No, but he had plenty of motive for killing the man *in whose bed the victim was sleeping!*"

The detective gave a low whistle. "Got the wrong man, eh?" he asked.

"I don't know. You stick around and see what you can uncover." Mason looked at his watch, then opened the door of Drake's car and said, "You can drive me down to the boulevard. I'll pick up a cab there."

"Headed for your office?"

"I don't know."

"You were there," Drake said, starting the car; "didn't you have a chance to do anything before the police came down on the place?"

"Nothing. There's another attorney there, a bird by the name of Duncan."

Drake deftly avoided a car which cut in, stepped on the throttle to beat a traffic signal and said, "Duncan cramped your style, eh?"

"I'll say he did. I wanted to find out something more about the murder, but that old fossil started messing around. Moreover, he claims he saw my client prowling around about midnight."

Drake said, "Watch your step, Perry."

"What makes you say that?"

"Just the look in your eye. You look to me as though you were pulling a fast one.

Mason grinned. "I'm pulling half a dozen fast ones," he replied. "I'm like a juggler on the stage who's got six billiard balls in the air all at once, only I'm not juggling billiard balls, I'm juggling dynamite bombs. I've got to keep moving."

"I'll find out all I can," Drake promised. "By the way, you wanted me to put a man on duty in Santa Barbara to relieve some chap who'd been watching a house up there. I got one of my men on the job, and everything's all fixed up. Just thought I'd let you know, in case you were worrying about it."

Mason nodded and said, "Good work, Paul. You'd better send another man up to work with him. I want her shadowed now, and I want as smooth a job as possible. And put a tail on anyone who leaves Kent's place after the officers get finished with their investigation . . . This is a good place, Paul. There's a taxicab. I'll take it. You can telephone from the cigar store there on the corner."

Mason flagged the taxi as Drake swung in close to the curb. The driver was alert and efficient, and Mason reached his office by ten minutes after nine. Della Street, as crisply fresh as a chilled lettuce leaf, perched informally on the corner of Mason's desk and rattled a barrage of information into his ears while he was washing his hands, combing his hair, and adjusting his necktie in front of the mirror. "Jackson telephoned just a few minutes ago. One of the judges had a jury trial scheduled at half past nine, and a default matter which he had to take up. So he called court at eight-thirty and Jackson explained the circumstances to him and got his signature on the final decree of divorce. I called the Winslow Hotel at Yuma to talk with Mr. Kent and Mr. Kent hadn't arrived. I called the courthouse. They hadn't heard anything of Kent. No marriage license had been issued for him this morning, and . . ."

"Wait a minute," Mason said, looking at his watch, "that information doesn't have any particular significance. The courthouse hasn't been open but a few minutes. It's just after nine and . . ."

Her calmly efficient voice interrupted him incisively. "It's after ten o'clock there. Yuma is on Mountain Time."

Mason closed the door of the closet which contained the washbowl and medicine cabinet, made her a little bow, and said, "You win, Miss Efficiency. What else?"

"I called up the airport, found the number of the plane Kent chartered to take him to Yuma, and got Drake's office to rush a Yuma detective down to the airport there to see if that plane had landed. I'm expecting a call any moment."

"I don't know why I don't stay out of the office and let you run the business," Mason told her. "You've handled things more quickly and efficiently than if I'd been here."

She smiled her appreciation, but continued to snap information at him. "They're trying their best to get you to handle that Anstruthers will case. I told them I couldn't give them an appointment but I'd see if you were interested."

"Who wants me to handle it?"

"The attorney who's representing the contestants wants to have you put on the case. He says he has it all prepared and all you'll have to do is examine the witnesses and present the case to the jury. . . ."

Mason interrupted her. "Can't take it,"

he said. "It comes up for trial this week, doesn't it?"

"Yes."

"I'm not taking on any additional responsibilities until I get this case straightened out. Tell them I'm sorry. Anything else?"

"Myrna Duchene was so grateful it was positively pathetic."

"Myrna Duchene?" he asked, his forehead puckered into a frown. "Who's she?"

"The girl who was swindled by the man who's at the Palace Hotel under the alias of George Pritchard," she explained.

Mason laughed. "I'd forgotten about her. She thinks my advice will work?"

"She's positive of it. She says she'll pay you just as soon as . . ."

"Didn't you tell her there was no charge for the advice?"

Della Street nodded. "I told her, but she just couldn't seem to believe it. She. . ." The telephone bell rang. Della Street lifted the receiver to her ear, said, "Hello," listened for a few moments and said, "Stay there. Report at once by telephone, if you hear anything of it." She slipped the receiver back on the hook and said, "Kent's plane—it hasn't landed at the Yuma airport."

Mason drummed with his fingertips on

the edge of his desk. "Now *that's* a complication," he said.

"Shall we report them as missing and have a search plane sent out?"

He slowly shook his head, said, "Ring up the airport, Della, and charter a plane. Have it ready to leave within half an hour. Don't tell them the destination. Tell them I just want to cruise around a bit."

"Charter it in your name?" she asked.

He nodded and said, "You might as well. I'll get more service in my own name, and if the officers are prowling around the airport they've found out about Kent's plane by this time anyway."

"You think they'll figure on a plane?"

"Sure they will—sooner or later. It's just a question of time. The butler spilled the information that they were going to get married and that I'd driven them somewhere in an automobile. It won't take much of a detective to put two and two together on that."

The telephone rang again. Della listened at the receiver, handed the telephone over to Perry Mason and said, "It's Jackson again at Santa Barbara. You take the call on this line, and I'll go out in the other office to telephone the airport."

Mason said, "Hello," and heard Jackson's voice on the line. "Hello, Jackson, everything okay? Della tells me you have the decree."

"That's right, the decree's signed and duly entered. What do I do now?"

"Who's watching the woman up there?"

"One of Drake's men. He relieved Harris."

"Della said you had something to tell me you didn't want to spill over the telephone."

"I didn't dare to. I'm talking through the courthouse exchange. I haven't been able to leave here yet. I'm afraid there may be a leak through the switchboard. Later on I can go to the main telephone office and call you from there."

"What's the nature of the information, generally?" Mason asked. "Use language that won't mean anything to an outsider."

"It relates to a consolidation of adverse forces."

Mason frowned thoughtfully and said, "Can you tell me anything more than that?"

"Apparently," Jackson answered, "arrangements are being consummated by which the plaintiff in this divorce action is planning to coöperate with certain other parties who are in an adverse position to

117

the divorce defendant." Mason made a little humming noise between his tightly closed lips. "You get what I mean?" Jackson asked.

"I think I do. I don't want you to spill any of that, over the telephone. Get down here just as quickly as you can.

"I can start right away."

"How about the others?"

"All ready to go any time I say the word."

"Where's Miss Warrington?"

"She's here with me. Harris is waiting out front in the automobile."

Mason said, "Climb in the car and beat it down here. Tell Harris to step on it. Now, Jackson, an unforeseen and unfortunate occurrence took place at Kent's residence last night."

"Can you tell me what it was?"

"A Philip Rease was murdered." Jackson gave a low whistle. "Therefore," Mason said, "it wouldn't be particularly advisable for Harris and Miss Warrington to jump into the arms of the police detectives until they've had a chance to prepare themselves somewhat."

"You mean you want me to bring them to the office before they . . . ."

"That's exactly what I *don't* want," Mason interrupted. "I don't want the police to think I've been coaching the witnesses. I'm in this thing deep enough already. And I don't want you to let on to them that you know Rease was murdered. But suggest to them that, because they may be questioned by Mrs. Kent's lawyer as to what happened during the evening, they'd better make certain their recollections check."

"Harris is the one who has the information concerning the matter I was trying to explain to you a few moments ago," Jackson said.

"About the consolidation of forces?"

"Yes."

"Just the same, I don't want Harris to come here before he's questioned by the police. Go over any information he has. Get Miss Warrington to take it down in shorthand and transcribe it later, if it's necessary. Do you get the sketch?"

"I think so, yes."

"Okay," Mason said, "get started. I may not be here when you arrive. If I'm not, wait for me."

He hung up the receiver, started pacing the floor of his office. Della Street appeared in the doorway. "The plane's all ready," she said. "I have a fast car ordered. It'll be at the curb by the time you get there." Mason jerked open the door of the coat closet, pulled on a light topcoat, paused to adjust his hat in front of the mirror. "When you get to the airport," Della Street instructed, "go out to the far end of the field. A two-motored cabin job will be warming up. I told the pilot to be *sure* to be at the far end of the field. I figured detectives might be hanging around."

Mason nodded, said, "Good girl," and made for the elevator.

The automobile which Della Street had ordered arrived at the curb just as Mason was emerging from the building. The driver knew how to make time through traffic. "Go to the far end of the field," Mason said.

"Yes, sir, I've already been instructed."

Mason leaned back against the cushions, his eyes entirely oblivious to the whizzing scenery. Twice he had to brace himself as the car swerved to avoid a collision, but the hour indicated on his wristwatch when he climbed into the cabin plane more than compensated for any inconvenience on the road.

Mason gave the pilot terse instructions.

"A plane took off for Yuma about daylight this morning. It hasn't arrived. Keep on the charted route to Yuma, and keep your eyes on the ground below as much as possible. I'll be watching."

"If we find it down, what do you want me to do?"

"Circle down as close to it as you can. Don't take any chances on making a landing unless someone's hurt and there's something we can do. If it's a crash and they're dead, we'll report to the authorities. If someone's in need of medical attention, we'll take a chance on landing."

The pilot nodded, climbed into the pilot's compartment. The plane roared into motion, zoomed smoothly upward. Mason looked down at the airport to see if he could make out a police car parked near the entrance, or see Sergeant Holcomb hanging about, but the plane swept overhead too fast for him to make an accurate survey. The ship climbed smoothly upward in a long curve, until the rows of white buildings glistening in the brilliant California sunlight gave way to the darker green of checker-boarded orange groves. Then, with a snow-capped mountain on both the right and the left, the plane shot through a narrow pass, rocked violently in bumpy air, and then flattened into steady droning flight. Almost as sharply as though marked by a line drawn with a ruler, the land of the fertile orange groves gave place to desert, a sandy waste dotted with greasewood, sagebrush and cacti. Over on the right, Palm Springs appeared, nestled against the base of the towering mountains. A few minutes more, and beyond the date palms of the Coachella Valley, the sun glistened on the Salton Sea. Mason peered steadily downward, looking first from one side of the plane, then from the other. He saw no sign of any grounded plane. The Salton Sea slipped behind. Below was a vast, tumbled aggregation of eroded mountains, huge hills of drifting sand, a country rich in its lore of lost mines, a hard-bitten, mirage-infested, thirsty country which had claimed a hideous toll of venturesome prospectors. The Colorado showed ahead as a yellowish snake winding turgidly through the desert. Yuma sprawled in the sunlight. The pilot turned to Mason for instructions.

Mason signaled him to go ahead and land. The nose of the plane tilted sharply forward. The droning roar of the motors died to a humming noise which enabled Mason to hear the sound of air shrieking past the plane. The pilot swung it into a long, banking turn, flattened out, gunned the motors once, then tilted the nose forward. A moment later the little jolts running up through the plane signified the wheels were once more on the earth. Mason saw two men running toward him, waving their arms. One of them, he saw, was Kent, and the other one was a stranger to him. Mason emerged from the fuselage. "What happened?" he asked.

Kent said ruefully, "Motor trouble. We had to make a forced landing. I thought we were going to be there all morning. We got in about five minutes ago, and this man from the Detective Agency met me. He telephoned your office and your secretary said for me to wait here; that you were due to land within five or ten minutes. She'd verified the time you took off from Los Angeles and knew just about when you were due."

"Where's Miss Mays?"

"I sent her on to the hotel. She wanted to freshen up a bit, and then she's going to the courthouse to wait for me."

Mason said, "We're all going to the

courthouse and get that marriage over with. Is there a taxicab here?"

"Yes, I have a car waiting."

"There's just one chance in a hundred," Mason said, "an officer may be waiting to pick you up when you get in that car. I want to talk to you before anyone else does. Come over here." He took Kent's arm, walked with him some thirty steps away from the pilot and detective and then said, "Now, then, come clean."

"What do you mean?" Kent asked.

"Exactly what I said—come clean."

"I'm sure I don't know what you're talking about. I've told you everything. The information that I gave you concerning Maddox is strictly accurate. The . . ."

"The hell with Maddox," Mason said. "How about Rease?"

"You mean my half-brother?"

"Yes."

"Why, I've only told you all about him. He's really incompetent so far as money matters are concerned. He's rather radical at times. His attempts to make money have met with failure, so he's naturally resentful of the chaps who have been more successful. He . . ."

"At approximately seven-thirty this morning," Mason interrupted, "Mr. P. L. Rease was found dead in his bed. Death had been caused by plunging a sharp carving knife down through the bedclothes into his body. The knife had apparently been taken from a drawer in the sideboard in the dining room and . . ."

Kent swayed, clutched at his heart. His eyes grew wide. His face turned an ashen gray. "No," he whispered hoarsely, speaking with a visible effort. "Good God, no!"

Mason nodded.

"Oh, my God!" Kent cried, clutching at Mason's arm.

Mason jerked his arm away and said, "Stand up and cut out the dramatics."

Kent said, "You'll excuse me, but I'm going to sit down." Without a word, he sat down on the ground. Mason stood above him, watching him with calmly speculative eyes. "When . . . when did it happen?"

"I don't know. He was found about seven-thirty."

"Who found him?"

"I did."

"How did you happen to find him?"

Mason said, "We found a carving knife under the pillow of your bed. After we looked at the blade we started an investigation of the house—taking the census."

"Under *my* pillow!" Kent exclaimed, but his eyes did not meet those of the lawyer.

"Did you," Mason asked, "know that Rease wasn't sleeping in his own room last night? That he changed rooms with Maddox?"

Kent's eyes, looking like those of a wounded deer, raised to Mason's. Slowly he shook his head. "Did he?" he asked.

"They exchanged rooms," Mason said. "Apparently you were about the only person in the house who didn't know the exchange had been made. The district attorney will claim that when you slipped the knife from the sideboard and went prowling through the house you believed the occupant of that room was Frank Maddox."

"You mean the district attorney's going to say *I* did it?"

"Exactly."

Kent stared at Mason. His mouth began to quiver. His hand went to his face, as though trying to hold the muscles from twitching. His hand began to shake. . . .

Mason said casually, "If I'm going to represent you, Kent, you've got to do two things: First you'll have to convince me that you're innocent of any deliberate murder. Secondly you'll have to cut out this business of putting on the jerks." As Kent continued to twitch and jerk, the spasm apparently extending all over his body, Mason went on as though he had been engaged merely in casual conversational comment: "Dr. Kelton says you don't do that right; that you might fool a family physician, but you couldn't fool a psychiatrist. Therefore, you can see how much you're weakening your case by putting on an act like that."

Kent suddenly ceased trembling and twitching. "What's wrong with the way I do it?" he asked.

"Kelton didn't say. He simply said that it was an act you were putting on. Now, why were you doing it?"

"I—er . . ."

"Go on," Mason said. "Why were you doing it?" Kent pulled a handkerchief from his pocket and mopped his forehead. "Go on," Mason told him. "Get up. Stand on your two feet. I want to talk to you." Slowly Kent got to his feet. "Why did you put on the act?" Mason asked.

Kent said in a voice that was almost inaudible, "Because I knew I was walking

in my sleep again and I was afraid. . . .
God, I was afraid!"

"Afraid of what?"

"Afraid I was going to do this very thing."

"What, kill Rease?"

"No, kill Maddox."

"Now," Mason told him, "you're talking sense. . . . Have a cigarette." He extended his cigarette case. Kent shook his head. "Go on and tell me the rest of it," Mason said. Kent looked around apprehensively. Mason said, "Go on, spill it. You won't ever have any safer place to talk. They may pounce down on you at any time now." He raised his finger and dramatically pointed to an airplane which, but little more than a speck in the sky, was heading toward the airport. "Even *that* plane," he said, "may hold officers. Now, talk, and talk fast."

Kent said, "God knows what I do when I'm sleepwalking."

"Did you kill Rease?"

"Before God, I don't know."

"What *do* you know about it?"

"I know that I walked in my sleep a year ago. I know I've been walking in my sleep from time to time ever since I was a boy. I know that these fits come on when there's

128

a full moon and when I'm nervous and upset. I know that a little over a year ago, while I was walking in my sleep, I got a carving knife. I don't know what I intended to do with that carving knife, but I'm afraid—horribly afraid . . ."

"That you intended to kill your wife?" Mason asked.

Kent nodded.

"Go on from there," Mason said, eyes watching the plane which was banking into a turn in order to come up against the wind. "What about this last flareup?"

"I walked in my sleep. I got the carving knife from the sideboard. Apparently I didn't try to kill anyone with it, or, if I did, I was prevented from carrying out my plan."

"What makes you think so?"

"The carving knife was under my pillow when I woke up in the morning."

"You knew it was there, then?"

"Yes."

"And do you know what happened after that?"

"I deduced what must have happened. I went in to take my shower and when I returned the knife was gone. At about that time Edna became very solicitous. That night, after I went to bed, someone locked my door."

"You knew that, then?"

"Yes. I wasn't asleep. The lock made a faint clicking sound."

"And you surmised it was Edna?"

"Yes. I felt certain it must have been."

"So what?"

"So when Edna started pulling her astrological stuff and suggested I see an attorney whose name had five letters, and was associated with rocks, I realized she was trying to put me in an advantageous position in case something horrible should really happen. So I ran over the names of the leading criminal attorneys in my mind, and made things easier for her by suggesting you."

"So you didn't fall for that astrological stuff?"

"I don't know. I think there's something to it. But as soon as she brought the subject up, I appreciated the advantage of coming to you *before* anything happened."

"And you suggested I get a doctor for the same reason?"

"That's right. My niece made that suggestion and I saw the advantages of it."

"And this shaking act?"

"I wanted to impress upon both of you that I was laboring under a nervous strain."

"So you put that act on to impress the doctor?"

"If you want to put it that way, yes."

"Why didn't you go to the police or put yourself in a sanitarium?"

Kent twisted his fingers together until the skin grew white. "Why didn't I!" he asked. "Oh, my God, why didn't I! If I'd *only* done that! But no, I kept thinking things were going to be all right. Mind you, I'd put that carving knife under my pillow and hadn't done anything with it; and so I figured that, after all, I wouldn't actually kill anyone. Just put yourself in my position. I'm wealthy, my wife wants to grab my property and put me in a sanitarium. For me to do anything would have been to deliberately play into her hands. I was in a terrible predicament. The worry of it almost drove me crazy. And then, after I consulted you, and saw the capable way in which you were going at things, I felt certain everything was going to be all right. It was a big load off my mind. I went to bed and slept like a top last night. I can't remember anything until the alarm went off this morning. . . . I was excited about my marriage. . . . I didn't look under the pillow."

The airplane, which had swept into a landing, taxied up to a stop. Mason, watching the people disembarking from it, said, "Okay, Kent, I believe you. I'm going to see you through. If you've told the truth, go ahead and tell your story to the officers. If you built this sleepwalking business up, as your wife claims you did in her case, to give you a chance to murder someone you wanted out of the way, say so now."

"No, no, I'm telling you the truth."

Mason raised his hand and called out, "Over this way, Sergeant."

Sergeant Holcomb, flexing his muscles, after emerging from the plane, started at the sound of Mason's voice, then, with Deputy District Attorney Blaine, at his side, came striding toward Mason and Kent. "What is it?" Kent asked in an apprehensive half whisper.

"Stick to your guns," Mason cautioned. "Tell your story to the officers and to the newspapers. We want all the publicity we can get. . . ."

Sergeant Holcomb said belligerently to Perry Mason, "What the hell are *you* doing *here?*"

Mason, with an urbane smile and a gesture of his hand, said, "Sergeant Holcomb, permit me to present Mr. Peter B. Kent."

—XII—

PERRY MASON PACED the floor of his office, listening to Paul Drake's drawling voice as it droned out a succession of facts. ". . . Sleepwalking looks like your only defense. There weren't any fingerprints on the handle of the knife, but Duncan now swears it was Kent he saw walking around in the moonlight. Duncan's hostile as hell. Don't ever kid yourself that that old windbag won't do you the damage he can. I understand that when he first told his story he said he saw a 'figure' sleepwalking. Now he says he knows it was Kent, and the only thing that made him think it was a case of sleepwalking was that Kent wore a long, white nightgown. He . . ."

Mason whirled to face Drake. "That nightgown sounds fishy," he said, "doesn't Kent wear pajamas?"

Drake shook his head. "Nothing doing, Perry. I thought we could bust Duncan's story with that nightgown business but there's no chance. Kent wears one of those old-fashioned nightgowns."

"I presume the district attorney's office grabbed it as evidence."

"Sure, they have the nightgown that was found on the foot of Kent's bed, presumably the one he wore."

"Any blood stains on it.?"

"I can't find out, but I don't think so."

"Wouldn't there have been?"

"The theory of the Prosecution is that since the knife was plunged through the bedclothes, the blankets prevented any blood spurting up on the hands of the murderer or on his clothing.

"That sounds reasonable," Mason said, "reasonable enough to convince a jury, anyway. What time was the murder committed?"

"That's a question. For some reason or other, the district attorney's office is trying to make it a *big* question, claiming that it's hard to fix the time exactly. They've told the newspaper reporters it was sometime between midnight and four o'clock in the morning. But they've been questioning servants to see if they saw or heard anything around three o'clock."

Mason, standing with his feet planted

apart, head thrust forward, scowlingly digested that bit of information. "They're doing that," he said, "to pave the way for Duncan to change his story. I'll bet you twenty bucks that they can fix the time of the murder within an hour, one way or the other, but Duncan said he saw Kent carrying the knife across the patio at quarter past twelve. . . . Paul, did that clock in Duncan's room have a luminous dial?"

"I don't know, why?"

"Because, if it did," Mason said, "they're keeping the time indefinite until they can convince Duncan that it was three o'clock instead of quarter past twelve. A man with poor eyesight, looking at a luminous dial, could easily confuse the two times."

Della Street, looking up from her notebook, said, "Do you think Duncan would do that?"

"Sure he would. They'll hand him a smooth line, saying, 'Now, Mr. Duncan, you're a lawyer. It wouldn't look well for you to be trapped on cross-examination. The physical facts show the murder *must* have been committed at three o'clock. Now, isn't it reasonable to suppose that it was the small hand you saw pointing at the figure three on the dial of that clock instead of the large hand? Of course, we don't want you to testify to anything that isn't so, but we wouldn't like to see you made to appear ridiculous on the witness stand.' And Duncan will fall for that line, go home, think it over and hypnotize himself into believing that he remembers distinctly that the time was three o'clock, instead of quarter past twelve. Men like Duncan, prejudiced, opinionated and egotistical, are the most dangerous perjurers in the world because they won't admit, *even to themselves,* that they're committing perjury. They're so opinionated all of their reactions are colored by their prejudices. They can't be impartial observers on anything."

"Can't you trap him in some way," Della Street asked, "so the jury will see what kind of man he is?"

He grinned at her and said, "We can try. But it's going to take a lot of trapping, and in some quarters it might not be considered ethical."

"Well," Della Street said, "*I* don't think it's ethical to let a client get hung because some pompous old walrus is lying."

Drake said, "Don't worry about Perry, Della. He'll work out some scheme before the case is over that'll get him disbarred, if it doesn't work, and make him a hero, if it does. No client of Perry Mason's was ever convicted on perjured evidence yet."

"You're trailing Duncan?" Mason asked.

"Yes. We're putting shadows on every one who leaves the house, and I'm getting reports telephoned in at fifteen minute intervals."

Mason nodded thoughtfully and said, "I particularly want to know when he goes to an oculist."

"Why the oculist?" Drake asked.

"I've noticed he keeps looking through the bottom of his glasses," Mason said. "They're bifocals. Evidently they don't fit him. A lot's going to depend on his eyesight. The D.A. will want him to make a good impression. Right now he can't read anything unless he looks through the lower part of his glasses and holds it at arm's length. That won't look good on the witness stand when a man's testifying about something he saw in the moonlight at three o'clock in the morning."

"But he didn't *sleep* with his glasses on," Della Street objected.

"You'll think he slept with binoculars on by the time he gives his testimony," Mason remarked grimly. "The district attorney's a pretty decent chap, but some of these deputies are out to make records for themselves. They'll give Duncan a hint about what they're trying to prove, and Duncan will do the rest. How about Jackson; is he back?"

She nodded, and said, "Harris overheard a telephone conversation between Doris Sully Kent and Maddox. I think you'll want Paul to hear what Jackson has to say about that conversation."

"Show Jackson in," Mason said.

She paused in the doorway long enough to say, "Do you think it's on the level—Kent's plane having motor trouble?"

"Yes, I talked with the pilot. It was just one of those things. He made a forced landing in the desert. It didn't take so long to fix the ignition trouble, but he had to clear off a run-way by grubbing out a lot of greasewood. It was just one of those things that happen once in a million times."

"Then Kent isn't married."

"No."

"That means Lucille Mays can be a witness against him?"

"She doesn't know anything anyway. Bring Jackson in."

When she had left the room, Drake said

in a low voice, "Would Kent have had any reason for making a detour with that airplane, Perry?"

Mason said tonelessly, "How the hell do I know? He said he had motor trouble, and so did the pilot."

"And he's your client," Drake remarked.

"He's my client—and yours," Mason admitted. "But don't be so damned cynical. I think he had trouble."

"Perhaps he did," Drake admitted, "but try and make a jury believe it."

The door opened to admit Jackson. Mason nodded. "Give us the low-down, Jackson."

Jackson was excited. "I've just been talking with the Clerk's office in Santa Barbara. I put my name, address and telephone number on back of that final decree of divorce when I filed it as attorney for Peter Kent."

"Well?" Mason asked, as Della Street unobtrusively slipped through the door and to her secretarial desk.

"The Clerk called me to say that Doris Sully Kent, acting through Hettley and Hettley, of this city, had filed an action alleging fraud on the court in connection with the entire divorce action, claiming there's been collusion; that Kent had persuaded her to file a divorce action; and that he'd lied to her about the community property, in that he had an undisclosed interest in a patent on a valve-grinding machine, and that he was a part owner in the Maddox Manufacturing Company of Chicago; that the patents controlled by that company are worth more than a million dollars and that they're community property. She also alleges that the final decree was a fraud on the court, and has filed an affidavit and application under Section 473 of the Code of Civil Procedure, alleging that she discharged her Santa Barbara attorneys and retained Hettley and Hettley; that she was under the impression the interlocutory decree had been granted on the fifteenth and told them such was the case; that they didn't have an opportunity to look up the matter until last night; that they sat up all night, getting the action ready to file."

"When were the papers filed in Santa Barbara, Jackson?"

"The action to set aside the interlocutory decree was filed around nine-thirty. They figured no final decree would be issued before ten o'clock anyway."

"And the affidavit and motion under 473?"

"Just a short time ago. They found out about the final when they got up there, and evidently prepared and signed those papers in Santa Barbara. The Clerk's office didn't telephone me until an attack had been made on that final decree."

Mason said to Della Street, "Send someone down to the Clerk's office here, find if they haven't filed a petition to have Peter Kent declared an incompetent person and his wife appointed a guardian."

He turned back to Jackson. "What about the business you were mentioning over the phone?"

"At three o'clock this morning," Jackson said, "Maddox telephoned Mrs. Kent and wanted her to pool her interests with them."

"At three o'clock in the morning!" Mason exclaimed. Jackson nodded. Mason gave a low whistle and said, "Give me the details. Tell me everything that happened."

"When I got your instructions I started watching Mrs. Kent's house.

"Have any trouble finding it?"

"No, I went right to the address you gave me. I stayed there until midnight and didn't see a sign of life about the place, except there were lights on on the lower floor."

"You mean you didn't see anyone moving around?"

"That's right."

"When what happened?"

"Around midnight Harris came up. It may have been a little before midnight; I don't remember the exact time. He told me he'd take over the job of watching, so I took Helen Warrington from his car, and we went to a hotel. Harris stayed there in his car. The night was unusually warm for this time of year, and Mrs. Kent had her windows open. Harris proved himself a darn good detective. When the telephone rang he made a note of the time. It was two minutes past three o'clock. He checked his watch with Western Union time the next morning and found he was one minute and five seconds fast, so that would make the time fifty-five seconds past three o'clock, and he made notes in his notebook of what she said."

"He could hear her?"

"Yes, it was still night and he could hear her voice through the bedroom window." Jackson pulled a folded sheet of paper from his pocket and read, "Telephone bell rings three times, then a drowsy voice says, 'Hello. . . . Yes, this is Mrs. Kent. . . . Yes, Mrs. Doris Sully Kent of Santa Barbara. . . . What's that name again, please? . . . Maddox. . . . I don't understand your calling at this hour. . . . Why, I thought that was all fixed. . . . Your lawyer has arranged a conference, and I'll meet you, as agreed. . . . You can get in touch with Mr. Sam Hettley, of the firm of Hettley and Hettley, if you want any more information. Good-by."

Jackson handed the paper over to Mason. Mason glanced significantly at Paul Drake and said, "One minute past three, eh?" He made little drumming motions with his fingertips on the edge of the desk, then said suddenly, "Look here, Jackson, when they filed that action at nine-thirty this morning they didn't know a final decree of divorce had been granted."

"That's right, yes, sir."

"Then they filed a motion, affidavit, and what not, under Section 473 to set aside the final decree?"

Jackson nodded again.

"Therefore," Mason said, "somewhere between the hour of nine-thirty this morning and the time those papers were filed they must have been in touch with Mrs. Kent and secured her signature. How does it happen your man on duty hasn't reported that, Paul?"

Paul Drake shook his head and said, "I've arranged to be notified by telephone, if anything unusual happens. The last report I had was about twenty minutes ago and he said Mrs. Kent hadn't been out of the house."

"She must have given him the slip," Mason said.

"If she did, she's clever as the devil. The house backs up against a barranca. There's a big retaining wall which encloses a back patio. The only way to reach the back of the house is by going past the front and around the side. There's a cement walk running around to the back door."

"An enclosed back patio?" Mason asked. Drake nodded. The telephone rang. Mason scooped the receiver to his ear, said, "Hello. . . . It's for you, Paul," and handed over the instrument.

Drake listened for a minute, said, "Are you sure?" then made a notation of certain figures in a notebook he whipped from his pocket, and said, "Okay, you stay on the job down there. I'm sending two more men down to coöperate. You stay with your couple unless they separate. If they do, you follow Duncan—he's the big bird with the bushy eyebrows. Let one of the other men tail Maddox." He slammed the receiver back on the telephone, looked at his wristwatch and said to Perry Mason, "She got out of the house all right. She's down here having a conference with her lawyer. My men trailed Maddox and Duncan to the Securities Building. They went to the offices of Hettley and Hettley on the fifth floor. My operative was starting back to the elevator after having followed them up when he met a million dollars' worth of blonde class in the corridor. She wasn't a spring chicken exactly, but she had clothes and she knew how to wear them, and she had a figure to put the clothes around, and she knew what to do with that. When my operative got down to the street, he asked his partner if he'd noticed the blonde doll, and it happened the partner had noticed her drive up in a green Cadillac. The license number is 9R8397."

Perry Mason scraped back his chair. "That's the break we want," he said to Paul Drake. "Get started. Put a hundred men on it, if you have to. Get witnesses to see

Mrs. Kent, Maddox and Duncan come out of that office. That'll corroborate the telephone call at three o'clock this morning, regardless of what anyone may claim on the witness stand, and, if I can prove that Maddox and Duncan were putting in long distance calls at three o'clock in the morning I can bust Duncan wide open on cross-examination. He said in his first statement that he saw the sleepwalker around midnight. Now, if he changes it to say that it was three o'clock in the morning, I can impeach him by showing that he and Maddox were putting in long distance calls at that hour."

"But perhaps Maddox put in the call without waking Duncan up."

"About one chance in ten million," Mason said, "but just the same, we've got to plug up *that* loophole before the case comes to trial. And I want to find out what she meant by telling him his lawyer had already arranged a conference. This is where your men get busy, Paul. Get on the job and keep me posted."

Drake crossed to the exit door, the casual indolence gone from his manner, his long legs covering the distance to the door in three swift strides.

——XIII——

PERRY MASON WAS studying the pleadings in the case of Doris Sully Kent versus Peter B. Kent when Della Street slipped in from the outer office and said, "Edna Hammer's out there. She's so nervous I don't think you should keep her waiting. She's crying and half hysterical."

Mason frowned and said, "What's the matter?"

"I don't know, unless it's the strain of having her uncle arrested."

"No," Mason said, slowly, "she knew this morning that they'd arrest him; but she was standing up to it like a little soldier."

"Better keep your eye on that woman," Della Street cautioned. "Tell her to quit carrying the world on her shoulders and let someone else do the worrying. She's emotional and if she doesn't watch out, she's going to have a breakdown and then heaven knows *what* she'll do."

Mason nodded, said, "Send her in, Della, and stick around."

Della Street picked up the telephone. "Send Miss Hammer in," she said into the

147

transmitter, and, as the door opened and Edna Hammer's strained features twisted into a perfunctory smile, Della went forward, and put her arm around the girl's shoulders.

Edna Hammer closed the door behind her, let Della Street guide her to the big overstuffed chair, sank into it and said, "Something awful's happened."

Mason said, "What is it?"

"Jerry walked into a trap."

"What sort of a trap?"

"A police trap."

"What happened?"

"He said the most awful thing without realizing what he was saying, and now he's going to have to skip out to keep from being a witness against Uncle."

"What did he say?"

"He said the carving knife *wasn't* in the sideboard when he went to get a corkscrew a half hour or so before he left for Santa Barbara."

Mason jumped to his feet. "Is Harris sure?" he asked.

"He says he is."

"And he's given that statement to the district attorney?"

"Yes."

Della Street, frowning thoughtfully, said, "Is that so awfully important, Chief?"

He nodded. "That's the one thing on which the entire case will hinge. Don't you see, if Kent had planned a *deliberate* murder, but wanted it to appear he was walking in his sleep, and particularly if he had any idea Edna was trying to protect him by keeping the sideboard locked, he'd naturally have taken out the knife *before* he went to sleep. In order to establish a case of sleepwalking, *we* must prove that he got up in his sleep, possessed himself of the deadly weapon *while he was asleep,* and committed the homicide without having the faintest *conscious* knowledge of what he was doing, and without forming any *conscious* intent."

"Perhaps," Della Street said, "Harris is mistaken."

Mason shook his head gloomily. "No," he said, "that's the one thing in the case that stands out like a sore thumb, now that I stop to think of it. He can't be mistaken. You see, Edna had the only key to that sideboard. I was with her when she locked the drawer. We, both of us, took it for granted the knife was in there. We didn't open the drawer to find out. In the morning the drawer was still locked. The butler came to Edna to help him find the key. She pulled a little hocus-pocus, produced it, and pretended it had been on the top of the sideboard all the time."

Edna Hammer sobbed into her handkerchief. Della, seated on the arm of the big chair, patted her shoulder. "Save it," she soothed. "Tears won't help."

Mason started pacing the floor. After several minutes, Della Street succeeded in calming the half hysterical girl, but Mason still continued the regular rhythm of his pacing steps. At length Edna Hammer volunteered a statement. "I'm fixing it up the best I can," she said. "Jerry's taking a plane. He hasn't been subpoenaed yet. He's going where they can't find him. Tell me, will it be all right to do that?"

Mason, his eyes narrowed, asked, "Has he given a statement?"

"He made a statement, yes."

"Did he sign it?"

"No, I don't think so. It was taken down in shorthand. Now then, before he's subpoenaed, can't he leave town, go to some foreign country?"

Mason said, "It's going to look like hell, so far as public sentiment is concerned.

150

The district attorney's office will play it up big in the newspapers. They'll intimate he's been spirited away to avoid testifying. Where is he now?"

"In his car, waiting down at the parking station across from your office. He has his bag packed and his reservation made on a plane for Mexico City. Then he'll go from there to . . ."

There was a commotion at the outer door, a woman's voice half screaming, "You'll have to be announced," then a man's voice exclaiming irritably, "Beat it."

The door burst open. Jerry Harris, his face grim, strode unceremoniously into the office, holding an oblong paper in his hand.

"By God," he said, "they got me—caught me like a damned fool, sitting right in my own car in the parking station in front of your office!"

"Caught you with what?" Mason asked.

"Caught me with a subpoena to appear and testify before the Grand Jury tomorrow morning at ten o'clock."

Mason spread out his hands and said, "Well, the district attorney stole a march on us. Hamilton Burger's nobody's fool."

"But," Edna asked, "can't he still leave? The plane leaves tonight and . . ."

"And they're undoubtedly keeping him under surveillance," Mason said. "They saw him come up to this office after the subpoena had been served. If he leaves the country now, they'll have me on the carpet before the grievance committee of the Bar Association. It was a poor idea in the first place. No, we've got to take this thing right on the chin. Sit down, Harris, and tell me about it."

"I'm frightfully sorry," Harris said lamely. "Thinking it over, I'm wondering if there's any chance I could claim I was mistaken. Of course, at first it didn't seem important and I was positive in my statement to the deputy district attorney and . . ."

"You don't stand one chance in ten million," Mason retorted. "They could almost establish the point *without* your testimony because Edna locked the drawer and kept the key. It's a cinch the carving knife *couldn't* have been in there."

"But they don't *know* I locked the drawer," Edna said. "I'll swear I didn't. I'll . . ."

"You'll tell the truth," Mason said. "Any time I have to depend on perjured evidence to acquit a client, I'll quit trying cases. If he's innocent; we'll get him off."

The telephone rang. Della Street picked up the receiver, then handed it to Mason. "Paul Drake calling and says it's 'important as hell.'"

Mason placed the receiver to his ear. Drake's voice, for once showing enough excitement to overcome his habitual drawl, said, "You wanted to know where Doris Sully Kent went while she was in Los Angeles. My men have been telephoning in reports. Right at present I'm advised that her green Cadillac is in a parking space across the street and that she's headed across for your office. I thought you might want a minute or two to put your house in order."

Mason cut off Drake's chuckle by slamming the receiver back into place. "Listen, you two," he said, "Doris Kent is on her way up. She's probably going to make me a proposition. If she meets you here or in the corridor, it might cramp her style. Miss Street will take you into another room. When the coast is clear, you can slip down the corridor. Edna, they'll probably be waiting for you at the street entrance with a subpoena. Don't try to dodge service. Be a little lady, smile, and keep your mouth shut. Okay, Della, take them into the law library."

Della Street was just returning from the law library when Mason's telephone rang and one of the girls in the outer office said, "Mrs. Doris Sully Kent insists that you should see her upon a matter of great importance."

Mason said, "Show the lady in," dropped the receiver back on the hook and said to Della Street, "Beat it into your office, Della, take notes on this conversation." He clicked a switch which connected a loud speaker inter-office telephone with his secretary's private office, then raised expectant eyes to the door from the outer office.

Della Street was just closing the door of her office when the switchboard operator opened the other door to usher in an attractive woman in her early thirties, who smiled at Mason with wide blue eyes. Mason surveyed her critically, took in neatly turned ankles displayed just far enough to arouse interest without satisfying curiosity, full red lips, accentuated by lipstick, fine-spun blonde hair. She met his detailed scrutiny with a tolerant smile. Without the faintest hint of self-consciousness, she walked across to Mason's desk, extended him her hand and said, "It was nice of you to see me." Mason indicated a chair. "I've heard a lot about you," she said, hitching the chair around so that she not only faced him, but he could see her crossed knees to advantage. "They tell me you're a *very* clever lawyer."

"My reputation," Mason said, "probably varies greatly, depending upon whether one talks with the plaintiff or defendant."

Her laugh was tinkling. "Don't be like that," she said. "You know you're good. Why not admit it? That's my trouble with lawyers—they're afraid to admit anything—always afraid someone's laying a trap for them."

Mason did not smile. "All right, then," he said, "I'm good. So what?"

There was a swift trace of uneasiness in her eyes as she sized him up, but the smile remained, a friendly parting of the full red lips, disclosing even rows of white teeth. "So you're defending dear old Pete," she said. Mason said nothing. "Can you get him off?" Mason nodded.

She opened her purse, took out a cigarette case, opened it and extended it to Mason. "No, thanks," he said; "I have my own." He selected one from his own cigarette case. She held her head slightly tilted to one side, her eyes expectant. Mason crossed to her and held a match to her cigarette. Her laughing eyes looked up into his.

She inhaled a great drag of smoke, expelled it in twin streams from appreciative nostrils and said, "I came to see what I could do to help." He raised his eyebrows. "Helping to clear poor Pete," she amplified.

"Just what did you have in mind?"

"I could testify that I had known for some time he was suffering from a progressive mental malady which made him irrational at times, particularly at night. On many occasions he has awakened and shown evidences of suffering delusions. I thought at first that he was trying to kill me, but, thinking back over it and calling to my mind certain matters which seemed trivial then, I can appreciate now that poor Pete was mentally a very sick man. He had a nervous breakdown in Chicago and never recovered from it."

"Anything else?"

She glanced at him with a slight frown. The smile was no longer in evidence. "What more do you want?" she asked.

"Anything you care to tell me."

"I don't think I'd care to tell you any more until I knew just where I stood."

"In what way?"

"Whether you were going to coöperate with me."

Mason said slowly, "I can't see where there's any question of coöperation, Mrs. Kent. If you have any testimony you want to give, I'll be glad to hear it."

"I can testify about a lot of things. Perhaps, if you'd tell me just what you needed in order to make your defense stand up, I could think of things which would be pertinent. You see, in the everyday contacts of married life there are many incidents which aren't entirely forgotten, yet which can't be recalled offhand, unless something refreshes the recollection. Therefore, if you'd tell me just *what* you want, I might be able to help you. You wouldn't need to worry about me on cross-examination. I can take care of myself."

"Meaning you can sway a jury?" Mason asked.

"If you want to put it that way, yes."

"Very well," Mason told her, "leave your address and I'll get in touch with you, if I can think of anything."

"Can't you think of it now?"

"No."

"I'd like to know whether you were . . . well, shall I say receptive?"

"I thank you very much for coming; but don't you think it would be better for you to have your attorney with you, if you intended to discuss matters of this nature?"

She leaned toward him and said, "I'm going to be frank with you, Mr. Mason. I'm glad you brought that up."

"Why?"

"Because," she said, "I haven't as yet signed any agreement with my attorney. I've been stalling him off."

"What do you mean by that?"

"He wants a contract for one-half of anything I get, if my action's successful. I don't want to pay him unless I have to, and I don't have to. Can't you see? My husband isn't in a position to fight me anymore."

"Why not?"

"Because he needs my testimony. If I can get him out of this murder charge on the ground he's mentally deranged, then I can set aside the divorce case. Then I'd be custodian of his property because I'd be his wife."

"I see all of that," Mason said, "but I

don't care to discuss it with you unless your attorney is present."

"Why?"

"Professional ethics."

"I don't see why you can't discuss my testimony."

"I can discuss your testimony but I can't discuss this divorce case."

"It seems to me, Mr. Mason, that you're very, very cautious . . . very ethical."

"I am."

There was no sign of petulance on her face, but she crushed the cigarette into an all but shapeless mass as she viciously ground it into the ashtray. "Too damned ethical, and it isn't like you," she said, and, getting to her feet, went at once to the corridor door without giving Mason so much as a backward glance.

—XIV—

IT WAS LATE afternoon. The big office building echoed with the sounds of hectic activity incident to the closing of business offices. Stenographers, anxious to get home after a grinding day in the office, click-clacked down the flagged corridor, their high-heeled shoes beating a nervous tattoo of rapid steps. There was a certain monotony about the whole hectic routine. Steps sounded in the distance, grew into added volume as they passed Mason's door, then paused before the glass mail chute as letters shot downward. Elevator doors clanged, the corridor was cleared of its human cargo, only presently to echo under a fresh barrage of pattering feet. As the clock chimed five, the sounds grew in volume. By five-thirty the building was almost silent, the center of noise having shifted to the street, from which blaring horns and shrill traffic whistles beat insistently upon the lawyer's ears. Perry Mason paced the floor, thumbs thrust in the armholes of his vest, head bent forward in thought. Apparently he was oblivious of all of the distracting noises. The door of his private office noiselessly opened. Della Street tiptoed to her secretarial desk and seated herself, waiting.

Mason hardly glanced up. "Go home, Della," he said. "There's nothing you can do."

She shook her head. "I'll stick around. Something may turn up."

Knuckles tapped on the corridor door.

She glanced inquiringly at Mason, who nodded to her. At his nod, she moved quickly across the room to open the door. Paul Drake said, "Thanks, Della," and gave Mason a quick glance. "Walking another marathon, Perry?"

"I'm trying to walk a solution out of this damned case."

"Well," Drake said, "perhaps I can simplify things a little. I've traced that call to Mrs. Doris Kent. It was sent in from a pay station in the Pacific Greyhound Stage Depot at 1629 North Cahuenga Boulevard. The connection was made at one minute past three o'clock in the morning, and the conversation terminated three and a half minutes later. Maddox put in the call, using his own name. It was a person-to-person call."

"Get photostatic copies of those records," Mason ordered. "You're keeping Mrs. Kent shadowed?"

"I'll say we are. What did she want here?"

"Wanted to have us give her the earth with a fence around it."

"Meaning?" Drake asked in his slow drawl.

"Meaning she wanted me to agree not to contest her action, but let her have the divorce set aside and assume control of the property as Kent's wife. She'd swear to anything necessary to have him declared incompetent. That, of course, would simplify our defense to the murder case."

Drake drawled, "Nice of her, wasn't it?"

"Very."

"Isn't the case against Kent pretty much one of circumstantial evidence?" Della Street asked.

Drake pulled a notebook from his pocket. "Duncan," he said, "has given out an interview to the newspapers. He swears absolutely that it was three o'clock when he saw the sleepwalker in the patio. He says the person he saw was Kent; that Kent had something in his hand which glittered. It might have been a knife, he can't be positive."

Della Street interrupted to exclaim indignantly, "How's he going to get away with changing his story like that?"

"Cinch," Mason said. "He'll claim that when he first told his story to the officers he was a little rattled; that he said the time was either quarter past twelve or three o'clock; that I didn't understand him correctly; that he didn't positively identify the sleepwalker as Kent because he was afraid his motives might be misconstrued; that the more he thinks of it, the more positive he's become that it was Kent, and that it makes no difference what we may think of his motives, it's his duty to tell the truth. Then he'll make a lot of wisecracks on cross-examination."

"You mean he's going to commit deliberate perjury?"

"No, the old fossil will think he's telling the truth. That's the hell of it. But this telephone call gives me an opportunity to take him to pieces. He wasn't asleep at three o'clock in the morning."

"Isn't there a chance Maddox might have put in the call without Duncan knowing anything about it?"

"I don't think so. I don't think there's one chance in a hundred. The fact that they were all in conference this morning proves that Maddox wasn't trying to slip anything over on Duncan. I thought at first Maddox might have figured he could cut Duncan out on the deal, but that doesn't check with the other facts."

Drake consulted his notebook again. "Here's something else," he said. "Do you know what time Harris claims he noticed the knife wasn't in the sideboard drawer?"

"It was some time during the evening," Mason remarked, "I don't know *just* when. Why?"

"Because," Drake said, "I think we can show the knife *was* in the drawer when it was locked."

"How?"

"By the butler. One of my men posed as a newspaper reporter and talked with him. He was all swelled up with importance and only too willing to spill everything he knew. He says that before he went to his room he went to the sideboard to look for something, and distinctly remembers that the knife *was* in the drawer at the time."

"What time?" Mason asked.

"He can't tell exactly. It was some time after the dishes were all done and put away, but, and here's the significant part of it, he *thinks* it was after Harris left for Santa Barbara. Now if that's true, the knife might have been missing from the sideboard, but it was returned before Kent's niece locked the sideboard drawer."

Mason frowned. "Why would anyone want to take it out and then put it back?" Drake shrugged his shoulders. Mason said, "That testimony doesn't make sense, Paul. I wouldn't trust the butler too much, myself. Harris *has* to be telling the truth. If the knife was in the drawer when the drawer was locked, Kent couldn't have taken it out. There was only one key."

"Of course," Drake drawled, "people *have* been known to pick locks."

Mason said irritably, "I don't dare to advance that theory, Paul."

"Why not?"

"A sleepwalker wouldn't pick a lock. If he had a key or knew where the key was, he might unlock the drawer, but I don't think he'd pick a lock. There's something about that which doesn't fit in with a sleepwalking theory. . . . Where did Doris Kent go after she left here, Paul?"

"Straight to her lawyer's office."

"Then where?"

"Then she started back for Santa Barbara."

"You have men shadowing her?"

"Two of them."

"You said there weren't any fingerprints on that knife handle?" Mason asked abruptly.

"None they can pin on Kent. There were prints, but they were badly smeared. The officers figure that either they were smeared by rubbing against the sheet and pillowcase, or else that you and Edna Hammer managed to 'accidentally' obliterate them. But there are no prints they can positively identify as Kent's. A newspaper man got the information directly from the fingerprint expert and passed it on to me."

"But if Kent's fingerprints weren't on it," Della Street said, "how are they going to hold him? Just because the knife was found under his pillow doesn't prove he's guilty of murder."

"The whole thing," Mason said, "gets back to Duncan. If I can break down Duncan's identification I can win the case in a walk. If I *can't* break Duncan's testimony, I've got to rely on sleepwalking. If I rely on sleepwalking I must prove how Kent got possession of that knife. If he took it from the drawer in the sideboard before he went to sleep it shows premeditation and indicates that the sleepwalking defense was a fake. If he didn't take it from the sideboard before he went to sleep then he couldn't have got it afterwards, because the sideboard drawer was locked and Edna Hammer had the only key in her exclusive possession all night."

Mason resumed his steady pacing of the floor.

"I thought you'd be tickled to death about the butler's testimony," Drake said moodily. "I figured that and the record of the telephone call would be enough to put the case on ice."

"The telephone call's okay, Paul," Mason said. "Something seems to tell me that's going to be a lifesaver, but I can't figure out the knife business. Somewhere along the line, there's something that doesn't click. There's something . . ." He came to an abrupt stop, his eyes wide with startled surprise. Slowly he gave a low whistle.

"What is it?" Drake asked.

Mason didn't answer the question immediately, but stood for several seconds staring moodily at the detective. Then he said slowly, "It's a theory, Paul."

"Will it hold water?" the detective asked.

"I'm damned if I know," Mason told him. "It won't until after I've plugged up a few holes in it."

He turned to his secretary. "Della," he said, "you and I are going to make a build-up."

"Doing what?" she asked.

Mason grinned at her and said, "I'll tell you after Paul Drake leaves."

"That bad?" Drake asked, slowly sliding

his body over the smooth arm of the big leather chair until his feet touched the floor. He stretched his long legs, reached the corridor door, opened it.

"Wait a minute," Mason called after him. "There's one thing you *can* do. I want to talk with Helen Warrington. Do you suppose you could get her in here right away?"

"Sure, I've got men trailing everyone in the case."

"That chap she's engaged to—Bob Peasley—runs a hardware store, doesn't he?"

"I think so, yes. Why?"

"Never mind why," Mason said. "Rush Helen Warrington up here."

"And that's all I'm to know?" Drake asked.

Mason nodded, "The less you know of what's going to happen, Paul, the less your conscience will bother you."

Drake drawled, "Hell, if I had a conscience you wouldn't even speak to me, let alone employ me." And, still grinning, he slowly pulled the door shut behind him.

HELEN WARRINGTON SAT in the overstuffed black leather chair directly opposite from Mason and looked frightened. It was the hour when there was a lull in traffic. The office workers had gone home. The tide of theater-goers and pleasure-hunters had not yet commenced to swell the downtown streets. The cream-colored, indirect lighting fixture in the center of the room shed a mellow light which showed her to advantage—a tall, straight-limbed brunette with large, dark eyes, midnight hair and very red lips. Her black-gloved hands nervously smoothed her dress over her crossed knees. "The question," Mason said, "is whether you're willing to do something for Kent."

"Of course I'm willing to."

Mason, staring steadily at her, said, "You're nervous."

She laughed, and the laughter caught in her throat. "Yes, I'm nervous," she admitted. "Who wouldn't be? A man tapped me on the shoulder, said he was a detective and that you wanted to see me right away.

Before I had a chance to get my thoughts together, he bundled me into a car and brought me here."

"You're engaged to Bob Peasley?" Mason asked.

For a moment there was defiance in the dark eyes. "Does that enter into the situation?" she asked.

"Yes."

"Very well, then, I'm engaged to him."

"Why haven't you married him?"

"I prefer not to discuss that."

"I thought you wanted to help Mr. Kent."

"I don't see how it's going to help Mr. Kent to have you prying into my private affairs."

"I'm afraid," Mason told her, "you'll have to take my word for that."

"We haven't married because of financial reasons."

"He has a hardware store, doesn't he?"

"Yes."

"Business poor?"

"He's overstocked with obsolete merchandise. He picked up a place at a receiver's sale. It'll take him months to get the old stuff turned into money—if it's any of *your* business."

"Take it easy, sister," Mason told her, drumming with his fingertips on the edge of his desk. She said nothing, but her eyes showed indignation. "You're living in Kent's house?"

"Yes, of course; what's that got to do with it?"

"Any detectives there now?"

"No, they made photographs, diagrams, and took measurements. They were there nearly all the afternoon."

"As your accepted suitor, there wouldn't be anything unusual in Peasley coming to call on you?"

"Certainly not."

Mason said, "Perhaps I'd better give you my theory of this case: Peter Kent is in a spot. Under the law, he can't be convicted of a murder until he's proven guilty beyond all reasonable doubt. I don't think the Prosecution could make a case if it wasn't for Duncan's testimony. Personally, I think Duncan's a pompous old fossil who's going to consider the facts of the case secondary to the appearance he makes on the witness stand."

"Well?" she asked, her tone more conciliatory.

"An ordinary witness might be trapped

on cross-examination, but Duncan's a lawyer. As such, he's more or less familiar with courtroom technique. He knows something about the ordinary traps he'll have to avoid. There's enough circumstantial evidence in the case to corroborate Duncan's testimony. If I can't shake him on cross-examination I'll have to rely on a defense of sleepwalking. That defense isn't too hot. I may get by with it, and I may not. A great deal will depend. The burden of proof is going to shift once I start to build up an affirmative defense.

"Now then, the former Mrs. Kent is very apt to prove herself a stumbling block to a sleepwalking defense. She may testify that Kent isn't a sleepwalker but is fully conscious of what he's doing when he pretends to be asleep, and uses the sleepwalking business to camouflage the fact he's a murderer. She can't give this testimony in so many words, but she can convey the impression all right."

"Well?" she asked, her voice showing interest.

"The murder was committed with a carving knife. It's a carving knife which matches a fork in the sideboard drawer in Kent's residence."

"Well?" she repeated.

Mason said slowly, "If the Prosecution should be able to prove that Kent had taken the carving knife from the sideboard drawer *before* he went to sleep, it would knock my sleepwalking defense into a cocked hat. The case is going to be close enough so that this would be the determining factor." He hesitated, to look at her searchingly. She returned his stare, her eyes curious but slightly defiant. "Now then," Mason said, "I'm going to be frank with you. I'm going to put my cards on the table. I'd like to get a carving knife which would be the exact duplicate of the knife with which the murder was committed."

"But how could you do that?"

"It would be possible," he said, "to duplicate the knife if a hardware man got the maker's name and the model number from the fork." He paused again.

She said slowly, "And because Bob Peasley's in the hardware business he could secure a knife which matched the identical set and then . . . Well, then what?"

"That would be *all* he needed to do," Mason said. "I wouldn't want him to do anymore."

"What would he do with the knife?"

"Give it to you."

"What would I do with it?"

"Give it to me."

"What would you do with it?"

He shrugged his shoulders, smiled, and said, "I might use it to lay the foundation for a cross-examination."

"Wouldn't this be a crime of some sort—compounding a felony—or something like that?"

"Possibly."

"I wouldn't want to get Bob into any trouble."

"I can assure you," Mason said, "that I would do everything in my power to protect you both."

"Bob," she explained, "is rather . . . well, rather peculiar. He's rather emotional, intent, and actuated by very high motives. He disapproves of the lives of what he calls the 'idle rich.'" Mason lit a cigarette and said nothing. Helen Warrington changed her position in the chair, laughed nervously and said, "You're putting me in something of a spot, aren't you, Mr. Mason?" He removed the cigarette and blew a smoke ring. She abruptly got to her feet. "Very well," she said; "when do you want the knife?"

"As soon as I can get it."

"You mean this evening?"

"By all means."

"Where can I reach you?"

"I'll be here in the office at ten o'clock."

She looked at her wristwatch and said, with tight-lipped determination, "Very well, I'll see what I can do."

"One other thing," Mason said; "I want to ask you a couple of questions."

"What about?"

"About Edna Hammer's bedroom door." Her face showed her surprise. "I happened to have occasion to drop into Edna's room," Mason said, "and I noticed there was an expensive spring lock on the door."

"Well," she asked, "what about it? Certainly a girl has a right to lock her bedroom door, hasn't she?"

"*Why* did she put that lock on there?" Mason asked.

"I'm sure I couldn't tell you."

"*When* did she put it on?"

"As nearly as I can remember, about a month ago."

"Did she give any reason why she was putting it on at the time?"

"No. Does a person have to give a reason for putting a lock on a bedroom door?"

"It's rather unusual," Mason pointed out, "for a person to put a spring lock on a bedroom door unless that person is either nervous or has been molested. Do you know whether there were any . . . well, let us call them unpleasant experiences, which made Edna feel a spring lock was necessary on her door?"

"I know nothing whatever about it. Why don't you ask Miss Hammer about it?"

"I thought perhaps you could tell me about it."

"I can't."

"Can't or won't?"

"I can't, Mr. Mason."

Mason inspected the smoke which curled upward from the end of his cigarette. "All right," he said; "be back here at ten o'clock with that knife."

"I'm not certain that we can . . . can duplicate the knife."

"Do the best you can," he told her. "I want a knife which looks as though it matched the set."

"Very well," she promised. "Understand that I'm doing this for Mr. Kent. I'd do anything for him. He's been very sweet and very considerate."

Mason nodded and escorted her to the

door. As her heels clicked down the corridor toward the elevator, Della Street, her face grave with concern, entered the office. "Did you take notes of the conversation?" Mason asked, switching off the intercommunicating loudspeaker.

She indicated the notebook in her hand. "Every word," she said. Mason grinned. "Chief," Della Street said, crossing over to him and placing her hand on his arm, "aren't you putting yourself absolutely in the power of this girl? She's crazy about this boy she's going with. The minute it looks as though he was going to get into any trouble, she'll turn against you like a flash." Mason got to his feet and started pacing the floor. "Please, Chief," Della Street pleaded, "your other cases have all been different. You were representing someone who was innocent. In this case you're representing the man who probably did the killing. The only defense you have is his lack of intent. After all, you know, we may be fooled on this thing."

Mason paused in his pacing, said, "So what?"

"So why put yourself in their power?"

Mason whirled to face her. "Look here, Della," he said, "I never tried a case in my life but what I didn't leave myself wide open to attack. You know that."

"But why do it?"

"Because that's the way I play the game.

"But can't you see what it means? . . ."

He walked over to her, slipped his arm around her waist, drew her close to him and said tenderly, "Listen, kid, quit worrying. Take me as I am. Don't try to make me the way I should be, because then you might find I was guilty of that greatest sin of all—being uninteresting. Let me give you my recipe for success—move fast and keep one jump ahead of your opponents."

"I know, but suppose they catch up with you?"

"That's no reason I should start looking over my shoulder, is it?"

"What do you mean, Chief?"

"I'm like a football player who has the ball," he said, "and is in the clear. Behind me are a whole swarm of enemy tacklers. Any one of them can tackle me. If I run the ball across the goal line for a touchdown, the stands go wild and no one stops to think of how I got it there. But if I start looking over my shoulder and wondering which of the tacklers may get me, I slow down enough so they *all* get me."

Her laugh was throaty and tender. She looked up at him with misty eyes and said, "Okay, you win. I won't doubt you any more. Perhaps, after all, I'm too much of a restraining influence. Let's carry the ball, and forget the ones that are trying to catch us."

"That's better," he said. "Keep moving. One jump ahead of the field and never look back, that'll be our motto."

She raised her right hand in a little salute. "Goal posts or bust," she told him.

With something of solemnity in his manner, he drew her closely to him. Her right arm slipped around his neck. Her half parted lips raised to his eagerly and naturally. It was Della Street who pushed away. "Somebody at the door," she said.

Mason, becoming conscious of the tapping knuckles on the panels of the corridor door, said, "That damned detective *can* drop in at the most inopportune times. Let the son-of-a-gun in. And get Edna Hammer on the line and tell her to be here at nine-forty-five on the dot. Tell her to come alone and not let anyone know where she's going when she leaves the house."

Della Street's handkerchief, wrapped around the tip of her forefinger, wiped lipstick from his mouth. She laughed nervously. "Remember, you're going to be talking with a detective. . . . Comb your hair down in back. I mussed it. Sit over there at the desk and act important. Pull out a lot of papers and look busy as the devil."

"What the devil," Mason protested; "it isn't a crime, you know. He'd be a hell of a detective if he didn't know a busy executive kissed his secretary once in awhile. Go on, open the door. To hell with all that funny stuff."

She opened the door, and Drake, standing on the threshold looked at Mason with glassy, protruding eyes. His lips were twisted into the perpetually droll smile which characterized his face when in repose. "Your hair's mussed up in back, Perry," he said tonelessly.

"For God's sake," Mason exclaimed irritably, "did you come in here to discuss my hair?" He ran his fingers through his hair, roughing it into a tangled mass. "Now it's *all* mussed," he said. "You can quit worrying about it. . . . And, if you could possibly manage to use an equal amount of detective ability on the problems I pay you to solve that you do in affairs which are none of your damned business, I could finish my cases in half the time."

Drake assumed his favorite position in the leather chair, crossed one long leg over another and drawled, "Then you'd only get half the fee, Perry."

"What's it this time?" Mason asked, grinning.

"I've been checking the various reports of my men. Thought you might be interested to learn that Maddox and Duncan went to great lengths to cover up their dealings with Doris Kent and her lawyers."

"Since when?" Mason asked.

"Since they first met in the office. She went out first. Fifteen minutes later Maddox and Duncan went out. They sneaked down the corridor, climbed two flights of stairs, so they wouldn't be seen taking the elevator at the floor on which Hettley and Hettley have their offices. There's a barber shop on the ground floor of the building. They both went in there and had shaves, manicures and massages. After they'd killed time for an hour or so, they went out separately. In going out, they stood in the door of the barber shop and waited until quite a crowd of people were leaving the elevator, then they mingled with this crowd. Evidently it was a prearranged plan, carefully thought out."

Mason drummed his fingertips on the desk as he digested the information. "Comb your hair back, Perry, it's driving me nuts," Drake complained.

Mason absent-mindedly drew a pocket comb through his hair. Della Street, who had slipped out of the office after Drake came in, returned to nod at Mason and said, "That party you asked me to call is coming in promptly at the time specified."

"Okay, Della, thanks," he said, without looking up, but continued to keep his eyes focused on the top of the desk as he drummed lightly with his fingertips. "The probabilities are," he said to Drake, "Maddox will deny putting in that long distance call then."

"Will Harris make a good witness?" the detective asked.

"I think so. He tells a straightforward story and he had the foresight to make notes. And he noted time to the second. He has every detail—and his notes show that the time coincides absolutely with the record of the telephone company."

Drake nodded. "That'll go a long way toward convincing a jury. Perhaps it would be better for you to let Maddox deny the conversation."

Mason said slowly, "That would be a sweet position to get him in; have him absolutely deny the telephone conversation, then flash the record on him and back the record up with Harris's testimony. What else do you know, Paul, anything?"

"Yes, you had the right hunch on Duncan."

"What about?"

"About the oculist business."

"Did he go?"

"I'll say he did. He's there now. He went directly from the district attorney's office to an oculist's office."

"At this hour?"

"Yes, evidently the D.A.'s office made arrangements to have the oculist there."

Mason chuckled and said, "Probably Duncan got to peering at the district attorney through the lower part of his bifocals and holding stuff out at arm's length to read, and they realized what a rotten impression that would make on the witness stand."

Drake nodded, said, "That's all for the present, Perry. I'll keep feeding you the facts as fast as I learn them."

Mason had resumed his pacing of the floor by the time Drake reached the corridor door. "A hell of a case," he said. "The facts dovetail together and yet they don't mean anything after they've been dovetailed. It's a crazy case any way you want to look at it."

—XVI—————————————

EDNA HAMMER'S FINGERS twisted the hem of her dress as she nervously crossed her knees and glanced from Della Street to Perry Mason. "What is it?" she asked.

Mason said, "I want you to do something for your uncle. Will you do it?"

"Anything on earth."

"This may be ticklish."

"What do you mean by that?"

"You might get into trouble, if you get caught."

She sat for a few moments, then laughed nervously and said, "How about you? Would you get into trouble, if I got caught?"

"Plenty of it."

"Let's not get caught, then."

"That's damn good philosophy," he told her.

"What do you want me to do?"

Mason said slowly, "Edna, I want to talk a little law to you, and tell you where I fit into the picture." She looked puzzled. "A lawyer looks at murders a little differently from the way other people do," Mason explained. "Murders are just cases to a lawyer. He doesn't know the people who are killed, he doesn't know the people who are accused. He's able to give better service that way. He's not blinded by sympathies and his mind isn't clouded by worries."

She nodded "Now then," Mason said "I want to ask you a few questions, just as the district attorney will ask them of you."

"What are they?"

"You are familiar with the particular carving knife which was part of the set kept in the top drawer of the sideboard in the dining room of Peter Kent's house?"

"Why, yes, of course."

"When did you last see that knife actually in the drawer?"

"I don't know. . . . I guess it was the time I put it in there after taking it out from under Uncle Peter's pillow. Do you want me to change my story? If you do, say so."

"You'll be asked that question in just about that way," Mason said, "and the only thing to do is to tell the truth, that the last time you saw the carving knife in that drawer was when you put it in there on the morning of the day of the murder. That was yesterday, the day you consulted me and persuaded your uncle to come in to retain me."

She nodded. "Now then," Mason said, "when did you *next* see that carving knife?"

"Under Uncle's pillow when you were with me."

"You are certain it was the same carving knife?" She nodded. "Now then, that illustrates my point," Mason asserted.

"What do you mean?"

"The district attorney will examine the witnesses just about that way and they are going to answer the questions just about that way. And in doing it, they are going to unwittingly commit perjury."

"I don't understand," she said.

"You don't know that the knife you saw under your uncle's pillow was the one you'd seen in the drawer. You surmised it was, because the knives looked the same and because you looked in the drawer for the knife, couldn't find it, looked under your uncle's pillow and found *a* knife there, which was of the same general appearance as the knife that was missing from the drawer.

"Then it wasn't the same knife?" she asked.

"I don't know," he told her, "but it is up to the district attorney to prove that it was the same knife and that it was the knife with which the murder was committed."

"Well, then," she said quickly, "I could say I wasn't certain it was the same knife."

"*You* can," he said, "but, before you get on the stand, he'll have called four or five witnesses, including the butler, and asked them, 'When did you last see the knife in the drawer?' 'When did you next see it?' and 'Where was it?' Then, having shown by inference that it was the same knife, he'll ask the question, casually—'Was it the same knife?' or 'You're certain it was the same knife?' or something of that sort. Now then," Mason said, "I can talk with you frankly, but I can't talk with the butler and the other witnesses because it would look as though I were trying to tamper with the prosecution's witnesses. Subpoenas have been served on them."

She gave a little gasp and said, "Come

to think of it, that's just the way they asked the questions of me when they took my statement."

"Exactly," Mason said. "What I am trying to do, Edna, is to point out a handicap under which I am working. No one *knows* that knife is the same. Everyone *thinks* it's the same. It's going to be important from our side of the case. The district attorney will sort of take it for granted that it's the same knife and all of the witnesses will do the same thing. Then, when I start cross-examining, *I'll* be the one who is trying to prove that it is *not* the same knife, and I won't have a leg to stand on. Now, what I want to do is to make the district attorney prove that it *is* the same knife."

"How are you going to do that?" she asked.

"By putting another knife in that sideboard drawer," he said, watching her narrowly. "You'll discover that knife tomorrow morning. Between us, we'll see that the newspapers find out about this second knife. The district attorney will probably think I planted it. He'll yell to high heaven that I'm guilty of unprofessional conduct, compounding felonies, tampering with witnesses and all that sort of stuff, but in order to counteract that, he'll *have* to start bearing down with his witnesses on the question of identification. In other words, he can't just make it a casual matter in which everyone will subconsciously take the identity of the knife for granted. You see what I mean, don't you?"

Edna Hammer nodded. "I think I understand." Della Street flashed Mason a significant glance. Mason motioned her to silence. Together they watched Edna Hammer adjust her mind to the situation. Suddenly she raised her eyes and said, "Who actually puts this knife in the drawer?"

Mason held her eyes. "You do," he said slowly.

"I do?"

He nodded. "And who discovers it?" she asked.

"Sergeant Holcomb."

She frowned and said, "Suppose someone discovers it before Sergeant Holcomb docs?"

"That," he said, "is something we're going to guard against. You take this knife, put it in the drawer and lock the drawer. . . . I believe you have the only key to that drawer?"

"Yes."

"You still have it?"

"Yes."

"You'll tell Sergeant Holcomb that I'm coming out in the morning at about eight o'clock; that I've asked you to let me in, and you ask him if it's all right for you to do so."

"And you think he'll be there?"

Mason laughed grimly and said, "You're damn right he'll be there."

"Will I get into any trouble over this?"

"You will, if you get caught."

"And you think it will help Uncle Pete?"

"I know it will."

She got to her feet, smiled and held out her hand. "Shake," she said.

Mason shook hands with her, nodded to Della Street and said, "Take Edna into the law library." As he saw the questioning look on Edna Hammer's face, he said, "I'm making arrangements to get the knife. I don't care particularly about having you know where it's coming from, because what you don't know you won't have to lie about. You'll wait in the law library. Della Street will give you some magazines to read. When we're ready, we'll let you know."

"When do I telephone Sergeant Holcomb?" she asked.

"As soon as you get the knife planted in the drawer and the drawer locked."

"That will be rather late, won't it?"

"Yes. But you can tell him I just called you and that you are to call me back to let me know. Don't worry about disturbing Holcomb. He'll be so tickled to think he's going to block me from doing whatever I have in mind that he'll fall on your neck and weep."

Edna Hammer's chin was tilted upward, her eyes steady. "I'll do it," she said.

Della Street escorted her into the library, returned after a few moments to find Mason once more pacing the floor. "Worried?" Mason asked her.

She grinned and said, "Nope. Go ahead and carry the ball, Chief. I'll run interference."

"Not worried about the tacklers?" he asked.

"Not a damn bit," she told him; "the goal post's ahead. On to a touchdown. Perhaps I can draw on my high-school days for a little encouragement. . . . How did it go? . . . Oh, yes: 'Strawberry shortcake, blackberry pie . . . V-i-c-t-o-r-y . . . Are we in it? Well I guess . . . *Mason's Law Shop*, Yes! Yes! Yes!'" She laughed up into his face, the carefree laugh of a woman who is sallying forth in life to encounter adventure side by side with a man to whom she has given her loyalty.

"Atta girl," Mason said; "there's another one. How does it go? . . . Oh, yes: *'Hickety hiff haff—rickety riff raff—Give 'em the horse laugh—haw haw!'* "

He had barely finished when a knock sounded on the corridor door. Mason nodded to Della Street. She opened the door, and admitted Helen Warrington and Bob Peasley. Mason motioned them to seats. "Get it?" he asked Helen Warrington.

"Bob wants to know something about what you have in mind."

"Just an experiment," Mason said. "I want a knife that's the duplicate of the one the prosecution claims was taken from the sideboard by Peter Kent."

"What do you want it for?" Peasley asked.

"An experiment."

"Can't you tell me more than that?

"No."

Peasley hesitated for a moment, then slowly, almost reluctantly, produced a roll of brown paper, opened it and disclosed a black, horn-handled carving knife. Carefully taking a handkerchief from his pocket so that he would leave no fingerprints on the handle, he crossed to Perry Mason's desk and deposited the knife on the desk. "That's it," he said.

"It looks like a dead ringer," Mason said, inspecting it carefully.

"It's exactly the same knife."

Perry Mason turned it over slowly in his fingers. "What do you mean by that?" be asked.

"I happen to know something about carving sets. I sell them. When I knew the identity of the carving knife was going to enter into the case and that Helen might be called as a witness, I noted the manufacturer's stock number, which was stamped in the shaft of the fork and looked it up."

"And ordered a duplicate set?" Mason asked, arching his eyebrows.

"No," Peasley said, "I had several in stock. You see, I sold the carving set to Kent."

"How long ago?"

"Two or three months ago. Kent didn't like the carving set he had and Helen was kind enough to say that I could get him one that would be guaranteed to give satisfaction."

"I see," Mason said, "thank you very

much. I feel that Mr. Kent is indebted to both of you, and when the time comes, I shall see that he is advised of your co-operation." Mason stood up, signifying that the interview was at an end.

Helen Warrington said, "You're certain Bob won't get into any trouble over this?"

Mason laughed and said, "Trouble is a relative word. It doesn't mean much."

Peasley said, "Frankly, Mr. Mason, I'm not certain that I am too keen about this."

Mason patted him on the shoulder and gently escorted him toward the door and away from the carving knife which lay on the desk. "Forget it," he said. "As a customer, I have a right to come into your store and buy a carving knife."

"Yes, of course."

"Well, that's all I'm doing now."

"No," Peasley said, "you're not *in* my store."

"If you'd prefer to go down to the store and open it up, I'll come in there and make the purchase," Mason said, laughing, but holding the door open for them. Reluctantly, Peasley moved out into the corridor. "Good night," Mason said, "and thank you again, both of you." He pushed the door shut and the spring lock clicked into position.

Della Street was leaning over the desk staring down at the knife. "What next?" she asked.

"A lemon," Mason said, "in that upper left-hand drawer of the desk, and we'll cut the lemon with the knife and let the blade stand with the lemon juice on it long enough to take some of the newness off, then we'll be very, very careful to wipe all fingerprints off of the knife. Then we'll give it to Edna Hammer. She'll be equally careful to leave none of her fingerprints on the knife."

"Just as soon as that knife is discovered, Sergeant Holcomb will try to discover latent fingerprints on it," she said.

"Absolutely," Mason agreed.

"And he won't find any."

"Of course not."

"Won't that make him suspicious?"

"Why?"

"Because a carving knife should have *some* fingerprints on the handle."

Mason made a little bow and said, "Now, my dear young lady, you commence to appreciate something of the position in which the district attorney will find himself."

195

"What do you mean?" she asked.

Mason said, "Bear in mind that there were *no* legible prints on the handle of the knife which was discovered under Peter Kent's pillow."

She started to say something when the steady ringing of the telephone bell filled the room with sharply insistent sound. "What line's that phone connected on?" Mason asked.

"The trunk line. While I was in here, I wanted to be sure we caught any incoming calls."

"Answer it," he said.

She picked up the telephone, said, "Hello," listened for a minute and then said, "Mr. Mason is here now. I'll tell him." She held her hand cupped over the mouthpiece of the telephone. "It's a man from the jail," she said. "He says that Peter Kent has just had some papers served on him and he's very anxious to see you at once."

Mason nodded. "Tell him I'll come right down."

Placing the carving knife on the desk so that the sharp edge was uppermost, Mason said to Della Street, "Bring in Edna Hammer and let's explain this thing to her before I start for the jail."

Della stepped to the door of the law library. While Perry Mason was carefully polishing all fingerprints from the handle of the knife with his handkerchief, Edna Hammer entered the room. "Why," she exclaimed, looking at the knife on the desk, "that *is* the same knife."

"Well," Mason told her, "there doesn't seem to be any identifying mark on either of the knives."

"What do you want me to do with this?"

He wiped off the blade on his handkerchief, inspected it critically, and rolled it up in the brown paper which had covered it when Peasley had brought it in. "Be careful not to leave any fingerprints on it," he said. "Put it in the sideboard drawer. Telephone Sergeant Holcomb and tell him that I'm going to be there at eight o'clock in the morning. And, remember, my dear, I *am* going to be there at eight o'clock in the morning, and I want you to let me in."

"And I'm to lock the drawer?"

"Yes. Don't let anyone know it's in the drawer, lock the drawer and keep it locked." As she reached for the paper parcel, he said, quite casually, "Why did you think your uncle was going to kill you, Edna?"

She recoiled as though he had struck at her. "What are you talking about?"

Mason took a quick step toward her. "You know what I'm talking about, Edna. You knew your uncle was walking in his sleep more than thirty days ago. You thought he was going to kill you."

"That's not so! That's false!"

"Then why," he demanded, "did you put that spring lock on the door of your bedroom?" She gave a little gasp, stared at him with frightened eyes. "Go on," he said, "tell me the truth."

"I . . . I . . ."

"You had a good enough lock on that bedroom door," he said, "but you were afraid your uncle had a key to it and you wanted a lock that he *didn't* have a key to, so you got a locksmith to install one of the most expensive locks money could buy, and you held the only key to it. Is that right?"

"No . . . that is . . . no."

"Then *why* did you put that lock on your door?" She stepped back away from him, dropped into a chair and started to cry. Mason said, "Go on, cry all you want to. When you've stopped crying, answer my question."

She raised eyes that were swimming with tears. "Why do you want to know about that lock?" she asked.

"Because," he said, "that's just the way the district attorney was planning to surprise you. He was going to jab his finger at you on the witness stand and make you act in front of a jury just the same way you're acting here. You can see what *that* would do to your uncle's case. It would make a jury think your uncle was a murderer at heart. Even if they thought he'd been sleepwalking, they'd convict him anyway."

"B-b-but that isn't the reason."

Mason stared steadily at her. "All right, then, what's the reason?"

"Jerry and I were married secretly a month ago," she said, eyes lowered.

Mason heaved a sigh. "Thank God for small favors," he said.

"What do you mean?"

"I was afraid you'd put that lock on because you'd known your uncle was walking around the house and were afraid of him."

"No. Honestly, Mr. Mason, that had nothing to do with it."

"Why didn't you announce your marriage?"

"We wanted to keep it secret."

"Does your uncle know?"

"No. He's the one we wanted to keep it from."

"Why?"

"He's a little eccentric."

"He approves of Jerry, doesn't he?"

"Very much. But I didn't want him to think I was going to leave him until after he'd married again."

"Well, then," Mason asked, watching her quizzically, "why all the haste?"

"Because," she said, laughing, "I'm in love and this is Hollywood, and Jerry is pretty much of a sheik. Lots of women are crazy about him. By nature he's fickle, and . . . Well, I just wanted to grab him while the grabbing was good."

Mason grinned and said, "Well, just so you didn't put that lock on the door because of your uncle's sleepwalking I don't care why you did it. But when I saw that lock I figured the explanation for it was more sinister than romantic, and I figured the district attorney was going to bust you wide open on cross-examination. . . . I suppose you have a key and Jerry has a key." She nodded. "And there are no other keys?"

She smiled and shook her head. "After all," she said, "I have only one husband."

"Anyone else in your confidence; anyone else know that you are married?"

"Not a soul."

"Okay," Perry Mason said, "take that carving knife, plant it in the drawer and, if the district attorney starts examining you about that lock on the door when you get on the witness stand or in front of the grand jury, show a little emotion just like you did with me, and then tell the truth and laugh and cry when you tell it, and make it plenty romantic." Mason nodded to Della Street, clamped his hat on his head and said, "I'm going down to the jail."

—XVII—

PERRY MASON, FRESHLY shaved, wearing a gray business suit which looked as though it had just been received from the tailor's, jabbed his thumb against the bell button of Peter Kent's front door. Almost instantly the door was opened by Sergeant Holcomb of the Homicide Squad. Mason's face showed surprise. "Rather early for you to be on the job, isn't it, Sergeant?" he asked.

Holcomb said, "Yes—meaning that it's rather early and that I'm on the job. What did you want?"

"I wanted to look over the premises," Mason said. "I had a couple of questions to ask of some of the witnesses. Any objections?"

"The witnesses are under subpoena for the Prosecution," Holcomb said; "you can't tamper with them."

"I don't want to tamper with them, I want to talk with them."

Holcomb held the door open, said, "If that's the case, come right in. I'll just stick around to avoid misunderstandings."

Edna Hammer came forward and gave Mason her hand. "Good morning, Mr. Mason, is there anything I can do for you?" Mason nodded.

"She's a witness for the People," Holcomb pointed out.

Mason whirled to face the officer. "Because the district attorney serves a subpoena on a person doesn't mean that person becomes sacred," he said. "The duty of a witness is to tell the truth. When the case is set down for trial, I'll subpoena a few of these witnesses myself. It just happens, Sergeant, that I am going to talk with Miss Hammer in private."

Holcomb said, "You can't tell her what to testify to."

"And *you* can't tell me a damn thing!" Mason said.

He took Edna's arm, "I think we'll talk in your room, Edna."

They walked down the corridor, Holcomb headed for the telephone. "What's he going to do?" she asked.

"Call the district attorney," Mason said, grinning. "How long has he been here?"

"Since seven-thirty."

"You called him?"

"Yes. I shouldn't be too friendly with you, should I?" she asked. "We don't want it to look like a frame-up."

Mason nodded, said, "You planted the knife okay?"

"Yes."

"What time?"

"About eleven o'clock."

"And locked the drawer?"

"Yes."

"Where's the key?"

"I have it."

"You're sure it's the only key?"

"Why, of course."

"How long have you been locking that drawer?"

"Since the other day when I found the knife."

"How do you know you have the only key?"

"Because the key was kept in the drawer. I took it out and used it to lock the drawer with. There was only one key."

"And the drawer wasn't ever locked during the daytime?"

"No."

"But you're sure it was kept locked all last night?"

"Yes, of course. *You* told me to lock it."

"No one saw you?"

"No one."

"And you didn't have occasion to unlock it later on?"

"No. Of course not. What makes you ask that?"

"I thought perhaps the butler might have wanted something in there."

"Why, no. It was late. He'd gone to bed."

"Okay," Mason told her. "Now wait until Holcomb leaves the telephone, then draw back from me a little and call to him. Tell him you'd prefer to have him present at any interview you give me, so you won't get into any trouble. Make a nice build-up. Think you could do that so it will be convincing?"

"Oh, I'd *love* to. I like to act a part like that."

"Go ahead," he told her.

She waited a few minutes until Sergeant Holcomb returned from the telephone to glower at them in angry futility. Abruptly Edna Hammer swung away from Perry Mason, took two swift backward steps, stopped and stared at him, as though puzzled. Mason moved toward her. She retreated a step as he advanced, then turned, impulsively, and called to Sergeant Holcomb. "Sergeant, may I talk with you a moment?" The eager alacrity of Holcomb's pounding heels as he strode forward was sufficient answer. When he had joined them, she said, "Mr. Mason thinks it's all right to talk to me but you seem to think it isn't. Wouldn't it be better, if you listened in?"

"He has no right to be present," Mason said angrily. "I have a right to question you as I want to, and he can keep out of it."

"But *he* seems to think he should be where he can hear what you say."

205

"What he thinks doesn't have a damn thing to do with it," Mason retorted. "You want to coöperate with me, don't you? Don't you love your uncle?"

"Yes, but I don't know what to do."

"Follow my advice," he said.

Sergeant Holcomb stood close to her side. "If *you* wish me to be present," he said, "no power on earth can keep me away. You've very properly indicated that this is what you want. Therefore, don't pay any attention to what he says. You're absolutely right."

She smiled coyly at Mason. "Really, Mr. Mason, I think it would be better this way. After all, you haven't anything to say to me that you wouldn't want Sergeant Holcomb to hear, have you?"

Mason said, "It isn't that, it's the principle of the thing."

"But, if it's all right for him to hear what you have to say, why not go ahead and say it?" Her eyes were wide, her voice ingenuous in its innocence. Sergeant Holcomb snickered.

Mason said savagely, "All right, I want to find out about that sideboard drawer and where you kept the key to it."

"I kept it on an elastic band around my wrist."

"Why didn't you put it in your purse or some other place?"

"Because I was afraid I might forget to unlock the drawer in the morning and that might cause some comment. As a matter of fact, I *did* forget to unlock the drawer but that was because the excitement upset me. You see, I took the key off when I took a shower. What I intended to do was to open the drawer just as soon as I wakened in the morning."

"So," Sergeant Holcomb said triumphantly, "it was an absolute impossibility for anyone to have taken the knife from that drawer after you went to bed, unless that person had another key or had picked the lock."

She nodded. "That," Mason said, "presupposes that the knife was in the drawer when you locked it."

"If it wasn't," Holcomb said, "it means Kent slipped it out before he went to sleep. So that doesn't mean any skin off of my nose one way or another."

"I'd like to see the key," Mason said.

She opened a purse, took from it a large key of peculiar design.

"You're carrying that key around with you?" Mason asked.

"Yes, I thought it would be better."

"But the drawer isn't locked now?"

"Oh, yes, it is. I locked it last night."

"Why?"

"I don't know, just nervousness, I guess. The thought of someone wandering around makes me . . . perhaps I hadn't better say anything more."

"Let's take a look at the lock," Mason suggested.

"If it'll set your mind at rest," Sergeant Holcomb remarked, "the police have anticipated your line of reasoning. We've had the lock examined by an expert locksmith. It shows no evidences of having been picked. There are no scratches on the ornamental key-plate, indicating that any sharp instruments have been inserted. There are no marks on the wood to indicate that the metal latch has been pushed back."

Mason shrugged his shoulders and said, "Well, I'll take a look anyway."

The three of them went to the sideboard. Mason examined the lock carefully, dropped to one knee to gaze at the upper edge of the drawer.

"Open it, please," he said; "I want to examine the inside."

Sergeant Holcomb stood with his hands thrust into his trousers pockets, his face wearing a smile of patronizing superiority. Edna Hammer fitted the key to the lock, clicked back the metal catch and opened the drawer. Mason, watching Sergeant Holcomb's face, saw that the detective didn't change his expression by so much as the twisting of a muscle, but Edna Hammer gave a little gasp. The open drawer disclosed a plush-lined receptacle for a fork and a knife. There was only the fork in the recessed receptacles. Mason bent forward as though to make a close inspection and Sergeant Holcomb leaned forward so that he might peer more closely, watching lest Mason should plant some clew. Edna Hammer's fingers clutched Mason's arm, clung to it frantically. "You looked in the drawer when you locked it last night?" Mason asked her, making his voice sound casual.

She nodded her head. Her eyes were wide with astonishment.

"Well," Mason said, "I guess that's all I need right here. Now, I'd like to talk with some of the other witnesses."

"Who, for instance?"

"Duncan and Maddox."

"They're subpoenaed to appear before the Grand Jury later on this morning.

"That's one of the reasons I want to talk with them."

"You can't talk with them unless they want to talk with you."

"Naturally. I'll ask them if they'll . . ."

Sergeant Holcomb said, *"I'll* ask them if they want to talk with you. If they do, all right. If they don't, you can't talk with them." He strode toward the left wing of the house.

Mason gripped Edna's shoulder, whirled her around to face him. "Didn't you plant it?" he asked; his voice savage in its impatience.

"Yes."

"Do you mean to say it *was* there when you locked the drawer last night?"

"Yes."

"Who saw you put it there?"

"No one."

"But someone must have taken it." She nodded dazed acquiescence. "Someone who knew the trick I was planning to play and decided to checkmate me on it."

"But who could have done that?"

"Besides yourself," he told her, "there were only two people who knew anything about that knife, unless, perhaps, you told someone."

"On my honor, Mr. Mason, I didn't tell a soul."

"Did anyone see you put the knife in there?"

"I'm certain they didn't."

"Where did you have the key last night?"

"I hid it."

"Where?"

"In the toe of an old shoe. I was afraid that . . . that something might go wrong, and I knew how much it meant to you. I . . ." she broke off as Sergeant Holcomb came striding into the room and said triumphantly, "Neither one of the witnesses cares to make any statement to you, Mr. Mason."

Mason sucked in a quick breath, as though about to make some retort, then shrugged his shoulders, said, "Very well," and stalked from the house, banging the front door behind him. He ran lightly down the cement walk, jumped into his car and sent it racing through the gears as he headed toward his office. He stopped at a drugstore, however, to telephone Drake's office. "When Drake comes in," he told the girl who answered the telephone, "have him send an operative out to search Kent's residence for a carving knife that's a duplicate of the one with which the murder was committed. Have the operative go through the place with a fine-toothed comb until he finds it. And he might start by looking under the top of that coffee table in the patio."

Della Street raised her eyebrows inquiringly as Mason hung up hat and coat in the closet. "Well?" she asked.

Mason said, "Mrs. Doris Sully Kent has tied up Kent's bank account."

"What do you mean?"

"She had a restraining order issued late yesterday afternoon, preventing him from disposing of any of the property. She's made an application to have a receiver appointed. The restraining order is effective until a hearing can be had on the receivership."

"But that . . . why, Chief, that would even keep him from paying you an attorney's fee." He nodded. "And he can't pay Paul Drake for detective service?" He shook his head. "And suppose a receiver *is* appointed, what then?"

Mason said, "It depends on who the receiver is and how the Judge happens to look at things."

"But Mr. Kent has lots of business interests. How can she tie them all up?"

"She's claimed that he threatens to dissipate his property, make fraudulent transfers and a few other things. She found a judge who was willing to listen to her."

"You mean he was willing to look at a stare of baby innocence!" Della Street retorted indignantly.

"You mustn't be unjust," Mason grinned. "Remember, she's only a helpless woman, who wants to do what's right. She states in her action that the alimony granted her in the divorce was a fraud on her and on the court. So she alleges in her complaint that she wants to have the fifteen hundred dollars a month discontinued."

"In other words, she wants to take all of Kent's property instead of just part," Della Street exclaimed. Mason grinned. "How can she get an injunction without putting up a big bond?"

"Our Code Section. Look it up sometime. Section 529 provides that there's no necessity for a bond whenever a court grants an injunction against a spouse in an action for divorce or separate maintenance.

"Then she can come into court and make any sort of perjured allegations she wants to and make it *look* as though she were really an injured party, and, when the judge tries the case and finds she hasn't got a leg to stand on, Mr. Kent can't do a thing about it?"

"Hardly that," Mason said, "but don't worry about that baby not having a leg to stand on. When she gets into court, the judge will realize she's got two very shapely legs to stand on. He'll see plenty of them, too. She'll make a good appearance on the witness stand. Kent won't; he'll be nervous, fussed and irritable. He'll feel that he's been unjustly held up. He'll stutter and stammer, he'll be so damned mad he won't be able to impress his side of the case on the court. Mrs. Kent, on the other hand, will be very calm, cool and collected. Accent on the collected, Della! She'll smile very sweetly at the judge and say that really, she doesn't want to do any injustice to her poor, dear husband; that she was tricked into filing the divorce complaint; that she realizes now he wasn't right mentally; that what he needs is someone to care for him; that he's mentally sick; that now is the time he really needs his wife and that her place is by his side, and she wants to be there."

"Chief, why don't you go into court and show her up?"

"Can't afford to," he said. "Kent will have to make *some* sort of a settlement with her. He can't afford to have his property tied up until this thing can be threshed out at a trial. He can't afford to have a receiver in charge; and he can't stand going through with all the litigation. He's nervous anyway. It would drive him crazy. By the time he got into court, she'd have no difficulty sustaining the allegations of her complaint."

"Isn't there anything you can do about it?"

"Buy her off, that's all."

"What makes you so certain she'd make a good impression on a judge?"

"Her past record for one thing. She's always done it. Remember, she's been through the mill. She's not an amateur when it comes to acting on the witness stand, she's a professional."

"And you're going to let her get away with it?"

"I'm going to buy her off, if that's what you mean."

"Then she'll help Maddox collect some more money?"

"Before she gets a settlement," Mason promised, "she'll tell the truth about Maddox."

"What do you mean?"

"I mean that she'll have to admit Maddox called her up at three o'clock in the morning."

"You think Maddox will deny that?"

"I'm practically certain he will."

"Why?"

"Lots of things. The way they're going about this business of pooling their interests, for one thing. What a fool Duncan is. He thinks he's gaining an ally. As a matter of fact all he's doing is letting himself be used as a cat's-paw. She'll use him as a club to hold over our heads. Then she'll shake us down and very sweetly throw Maddox overboard in order to make her own settlement."

"When are you going to settle with her?"

"The Grand Jury is going to indict Kent on a murder charge this morning," Mason said. "The district attorney will make a play for an immediate trial. I'm going to consent. Maddox and Duncan will testify to a bunch of stuff. Then I'll tear into Maddox, asking him where he was and what he was doing at three o'clock in the morning. He'll stall around and either won't answer or else will lie. Then I'll take Doris Sully Kent out and make a settlement with her. I'll explain to her that, if I could prove Maddox *did* telephone her, it possibly would clear up Mr. Kent's difficulties so he would feel able to make a substantial cash settlement. Then Harris can go on the stand and testify to the telephone conversation and she'll go on the stand and corroborate it. That will make Maddox out a liar."

"Of course, she'd have to swear she recognized Maddox's voice and apparently it was the first time she'd heard from him."

"Technically, yes, practically, no. All I need to do is to put Harris on the stand, let him tell his story, call her to the stand and let it appear she's a hostile witness. I'll ask her if Maddox didn't telephone her at that time. They'll object. Then I'll ask her if *some* man didn't telephone at that time who *said* he was Maddox. They'll probably object to that. The court may sustain them, unless she can testify she recognized Maddox's voice. I'll pretend to be very exasperated then suddenly ask her, 'Madam, what were *you* doing at the time the murder was committed, on the morning of the fourteenth—were you, or were you not, at that time holding a telephone in your hand and talking with some person over long distance?' She'll give a very faint and apparently reluctant 'yes' and that'll be just about all the jury needs. I'll dismiss her from the witness stand. The district attorney will be afraid to cross-examine her. Then I'll introduce photostatic copies of the telephone company records."

"How much is a settlement going to cost Peter Kent?" she asked.

"He's told me to go up to a hundred-and-fifty thousand dollars, if I have to."

"Will you have to?"

"I don't think so. I hope not, but she's greedy. I'll stall around a while before I make her any offer."

"You'll deal through her attorney?"

"Yes."

"Won't that make it more expensive?"

"Yes."

"Why not deal directly with her?"

"It wouldn't be ethical."

"Somehow," Della Street said, "she doesn't

impress me as being a woman who would want to pay a big slice of what she receives to an attorney."

Mason was about to say something when the telephone bell rang and Della Street, picking up the receiver, cupped her hand over the transmitter and said, "It's Mrs. Doris Sully Kent. She's in the office now. She wants to see you, and says to tell you that she has discharged her attorneys, so that at present she has no one representing her." Mason gave a low whistle. "So what do we do?" Della Street asked.

Mason made an exaggerated bow in the direction of the outer office. "The little woman is clever," he said; "we see her."

"You want me to take down everything she says?"

"Yes. Through the interoffice loud-speaking arrangement, however. You wait in the law library and keep a line open to this office. Take down everything that's said. By the way, Della, have you ever seen her?"

"No."

"Well, manage to get a look at her when she comes in, but keep out of sight yourself."

Della Street nodded, scooped up notebook and pencils, and headed for the outer office. Mason snapped the switch which operated the interoffice loud-speaking arrangement and said in a conversational tone of voice, "Tell Mrs. Kent I can give her just five minutes." He lit a cigarette and was apparently concentrating on the contents of a law book so that he didn't hear her when she stepped into the room.

She coughed, Mason raised his eyes, said, "Good morning," waved his hand in the general direction of a chair, and returned to a perusal of the book.

She hesitated for a moment, then walked toward his desk, stood very close to him and said, "If you're busy, I won't bother you."

"That's all right," he said without looking up, "I'll see you in a minute. Don't interrupt me."

She continued to stand very close to him. "I came as a friend," she said. Her voice was seductively low.

Mason sighed, pushed the book away, and pointed to a chair. "Go over there and sit down. Tell me about it and give me all the facts so I don't have to ask for a lot of explanations." She hesitated a moment, then with a little petulant shrug of her shoulders, seated herself, crossed her knees, and smiled at him. "Go ahead," he told her.

"I've discharged my attorney."

"Paid him off?"

"Does that make any difference?"

"It might. Particularly if he has any papers which belong to you."

"I've reached a complete understanding with him."

"Very well; what else?"

"I want to talk with you."

"Go ahead, I'm listening."

"Has it ever occurred to you, Mr. Mason," she asked, dropping her seductive manner, "that I hold the whip hand?"

"No," he said, "it hasn't."

"Well, I do." He made a gesture, as though to reach for his law book and she started a rapid fire of conversation. "Do you know what it'll mean, if I get on the stand and swear that Peter got a carving knife and tried to kill me; that he *said* he was walking in his sleep, but that I knew he was lying? Well, I don't want to do that. I want to help Peter. But, if Peter is going to fight me. I'll have to fight Peter."

"Go on," Mason said.

"I just want you to understand I'm looking out for myself."

"I understand that."

"And don't think I can't do it!"

"I also understand you're fairly good at that."

"Well, I want to know where I stand."

"I'm sure I can't tell you."

"Yes, you can. You're Peter's lawyer. I know Peter well enough to know that when it comes to standing up to a real knock-down-and-drag-out fight, he won't do it. He's too nervous. We can settle this thing. He'll want to settle. He's got to settle."

"What do you want, an income or a cash settlement?"

"Neither. I want to have Peter take me back as his wife. I want to stand by him during this period of adversity. I want him to let me take my place by his side."

"So, after a few months, you can begin all over again and get a larger settlement and a larger chunk of alimony?" Mason asked.

"That's unkind, Mr. Mason. You have no right to say that. That *isn't* what I want. I want to be Peter's wife."

"Knowing," Mason said acidly, "that he's in love and wants to marry, you decide that you can throw more monkey wrenches into the machinery by keeping him tied up to you. He'll eventually pay more to buy his freedom."

She produced a lace handkerchief, slowly, dramatically. Her eyes blinked rapidly, filled with tears, the corners of her lips quivered, then with a little, inarticulate cry, she raised the handkerchief to her eyes. Her shoulders heaved with sobs.

Mason watched her unemotionally. "How much for a cash settlement?" he asked.

"I don't want a c-c-cash settlement."

"How much for a monthly income?"

"I don't want a m-m-monthly income. I w-w-want P-P-Peter. I w-w-want to help him. I w-w-want to t-t-testify that he's not right mentally. I hope he c-c-can be c-c-cured. But, if he c-c-can't, I want to s-s-stand by him."

Mason's face showed indignation. He got to his feet, strode toward the sobbing figure and reached out as though to jerk the handkerchief from her eyes, then as he stood there, his eyes suddenly narrowed in thought. He stood in frowning concentration for a moment, then turned back to the desk and surreptitiously slid his forefinger to the push button which summoned Della Street to his office. A moment later, as his puzzled secretary noiselessly opened the door from the law library, Mason moved his hands about his head in a pantomime, indicating a hat. Then he made gestures about his shoulders, imitating the motions of one holding a coat collar tightly about the throat. Della Street frowned in a perplexed attempt to gather his meaning. Mrs. Kent continued to sob into her handkerchief. Mason walked over to her, patted her shoulder. "There, there, my dear," he said sympathetically, "I didn't mean to be harsh with you. Perhaps I've misunderstood you. *Get your hat and coat and come back.*"

She peeked up at him from around the side of her handkerchief. "My hat and coat?" she asked, puzzled.

"Oh, pardon me," Mason said hastily; "what I meant was that I wanted you to return when you weren't so emotionally upset." Della Street noiselessly closed the door to the law library.

"You were m-m-mean to me," Doris Kent sniffled into her handkerchief.

"I'm sorry," Mason said, patting her shoulder; "I'm upset this morning and perhaps I did you an injustice." She dried her tears, blew her nose, sighed tremulously and put the handkerchief in her purse. Her eyes glinted with the remains of unmistakably genuine tears. "Do you," he asked casually, "still have keys to Peter Kent's residence?"

"Of course. I haven't used them for a year, however. Why did you ask?"

"Nothing in particular. I just wondered."

"Well, does it make any difference?"

"Not necessarily. What's your attitude going to be toward Maddox?"

She raised her eyebrows and said, "Maddox? . . . Maddox? . . . I don't believe I know him."

"Maddox, from Chicago," he said; "you know, the Maddox Manufacturing Company."

"Oh, that was something my lawyer discovered about my husband's property. He said that the Maddox Manufacturing Company had patents that were worth millions and Peter had deliberately concealed the information from me, so he wouldn't appear to be so wealthy when my divorce action was filed. But that's all passed now."

"But don't you know Maddox personally?" Mason asked.

She looked at him with wide, astonished eyes, and said, "Certainly not."

"Nor Duncan, his attorney?"

She shook her head, her face the picture of surprise.

"I thought you talked with Maddox over the telephone."

"Why, whatever gave you that idea?"

He shrugged his shoulders and said, "Skip it."

"No, but I want to know. I really *am* interested, Mr. Mason, because I feel that someone has been lying about me. Perhaps that's why Peter feels about me as he does."

The door from the law library silently opened. Della Street, attired in a fur coat, gloved hands holding a black purse, a close-fitting hat tilted rakishly at an angle, raised inquiring eyebrows at Mason. He nodded. She took a dubious step into the room. Mason strode toward her, "Why, Miss Street," he exclaimed, "Why, my *dear* Miss Street." Doris Kent stared frigidly. "Why, how did you get in here?" Mason asked, coming toward her. "I'm busy. I wasn't to be interrupted. I haven't forgotten about your appointment . . . I . . ."

Della Street came breezily toward him, gave him her gloved hand. "I'm sorry, if I intruded, Mr. Mason," she said, "but I knew what a stickler you were for accuracy in appointments. Some girl in the outer office told me to go in the law library and wait because you were busy. Since I had a most definite appointment, and knowing how important my matter was, I simply couldn't believe her. Therefore, after I'd waited a few minutes, I opened the door. I'm very, very sorry."

"It just happened," Mason explained, "that another matter interfered . . ." He broke off and motioned toward Doris Kent, who got slowly to her feet.

"I'm afraid," Della Street said, watching Mason's face, "that I must insist upon my appointment, however, Mr. Mason. I have only a very few minutes. You remember, you told me over the telephone that I wouldn't have to wait. I know it was wrong for me to break in, but, after all, an appointment is an appointment."

Mason's manner was embarrassed. He turned to Doris Kent and said, "I'm very sorry. You'll remember, I told you I could only give you a few minutes. I've had this appointment with Miss Street . . ."

"It's quite all right," Doris Kent said, throwing up her chin. "I'll come back."

Mason caught Della Street's eye, jerked his head toward Doris Kent. Della moved toward her.

"I'm sure you'll excuse me, won't you, my dear, but I have only a few minutes available."

Mrs. Kent smiled graciously. "Not at all," she said, "don't mention it. I realize how busy Mr. Mason is. After all, I think he understands my position and . . . ."

"Where can I get in touch with you?" Mason asked.

"At the Lafitte Hotel. I'll be there for the next two or three days."

Mason gave a start of surprise and said, "Why, that's your hotel, isn't it, Miss Street?"

"Yes, I'm staying there. It's very nice," Della Street remarked amiably.

Mason escorted Doris Kent to the corridor. "I'm very sorry," he said, "that this happened. She really shouldn't have opened the door to my private office. But she had the appointment. She's rather wealthy and quite impulsive. . . ."

"I understand perfectly," Doris Kent said, and, turning, gave him her hand. "After all," she said, "we can be friends, can't we?" and her eyes were filled with promise.

Mason patted her hand, turned and reentered his office. Della Street, looking up at him anxiously, said, "Did I muff it?"

"No," he told her, "You did nobly. Just exactly what I wanted."

"What was the big idea?"

"Get a bunch of glad rags and move into the Lafitte Hotel. Keep sticking around until you see Doris Kent. Go over and get acquainted with her. Tell her how sorry you were that you interrupted her conference: that you realized afterward you had no right to bust in on her and that you don't know what made you do it. Tell her I'm usually so careful about appointments, that you felt there'd been a mistake made by someone in the office; that you were in a hurry and simply had to see me."

"Then what?" she asked. "Surely, Chief, you don't think she'd become confidential and tell me anything which would damage her side of the case? Particularly when she knows that I know you, and . . ."

He chuckled. "What's the name of the girl who got gypped in the love racket?"

She frowned at him and asked, "What the devil are you talking about, Chief?"

"You know, the girl that wanted me to handle her case? She got gypped for five thousand dollars . . ."

"Oh, you mean Myrna Duchene."

"That's the one," he told her. "Where's her boyfriend?"

"He's at the Palace Hotel. Going under the name of George Pritchard."

"Okay," Mason said, "now you go to the Lafitte Hotel. Cultivate a speaking acquaintanceship with Mrs. Kent. Get Myrna Duchene to point out this love pirate to you. I presume he's the type that makes a girl's heart go pitty-pat, isn't he?"

"I gather that he is," Della Street said, puzzled. "I saw a photograph of him. He certainly looked like the answer to a maiden's prayer."

Mason said, "Scrape an acquaintance with him. Hand him a hard luck story about having lost your money but don't do that until after he's called on you at your hotel. Keep him calling there until you have an opportunity to point out Mrs. Kent to him as a very wealthy widow. And, if you can possibly work it, you'll introduce him to Mrs. Kent . . ."

Her eyes showed swift comprehension. "And let nature take its course?" she interrupted.

Mason bowed and smiled. "Exactly," he said.

THE SIGN WHICH stretched across the front of the store was relatively new. "PEASLEY HARDWARE CO." it read. The rest of the store was old. In the dusty, drab show windows an attempt had been made to put new wine into old bottles. Various tools had been arranged in geometric designs. Wooden steps had been covered with green cloth and used to display stock to advantage, but, for the most part, that stock gave unmistakable evidences of having been on display for some time. Perry Mason pushed his way through the door. Obviously new electric fixtures showered brilliant illumination over the counters; but the gloomy walls drank up the light and left only drab dregs for the eye.

Bob Peasley came walking briskly forward from a little office in the rear. When he was close enough to recognize Mason his step faltered appreciably, then he squared his shoulders and came up, giving Mason a forced smile of greeting. "How do you do, Mr. Mason? This is indeed a pleasure!"

"Hello, Peasley. Nice place you have here."

"Think so? Glad you like it."

"How long have you been here?"

"Not so long. I picked it up cheap at a receiver's sale. I'm trying to get rid of some of the old stock now. Then I either want to move or else have the whole interior done over."

"A lease?" Mason asked.

"Yes, and it's rather an advantageous lease. But I can't get the landlord to do anything toward fixing up. I have the right to make changes and improvements at my own expense, however."

"Going to start soon?"

"Soon as I can move some of the old stock and get some cash."

"How's it going?"

"Fair. I'm going to have a big clearance sale in about thirty days. I really don't know all that I have here yet. There wasn't any current inventory, and the one the receiver made was just a make-shift. It was so dark in here that I honestly don't know how a customer ever had a chance to find his way in. I put in new lights, but, somehow, it still seems cobwebby." Peasley glanced cautiously over his shoulder, lowered his voice and said, "How was the carving knife?"

"Excellent," Mason answered. "Just exactly what I wanted." Peasley fidgeted uncomfortably. "What's the matter," Mason inquired, "anything?" Peasley shook his head. "Seen Helen Warrington lately?"

"Last night," Peasley answered. "Why? Nothing wrong is there?" His eyes didn't meet Mason's.

"Seen Miss Hammer lately?"

"No."

"Harris?"

Peasley's face flushed. "Any particular reason why you should ask me about him?" he asked.

"Just wondering," Mason said.

"No, I haven't seen him."

"Well," Mason said, "whom have you seen?"

"What do you mean?"

Mason placed a fatherly hand on the young man's shoulder. "Look here, Peasley," he said, "something's gone wrong. What is it?"

Peasley hesitated a moment then said in a mumbled undertone, "Nothing."

He casually moved so that Mason's hand dropped from his shoulder. His manner turned surly. Mason said slowly, "*I* think I've been double-crossed. What do *you* know about that?"

Peasley's eyes flared. "Not a damn thing," he said, "and I don't know what you're coming here for."

"Talk with anyone about the knife?" Mason asked, casually, and almost cheerfully.

Peasley said, "Say, what the devil *are* you after?"

"Just wanted to find out," Mason remarked. Peasley kept quiet. "Have you?" Mason asked.

"I can't tell you."

"Why can't you?"

"Because . . . because I can't."

"Helen Warrington tell you not to?" Mason asked. Peasley was silent. Mason laughed and said, "Don't make such a mystery of it. Sergeant Holcomb knows about it so there's no reason why you shouldn't tell the world."

Peasley's face showed a peculiar change of expression. "You know about that?" he asked.

"What, about Sergeant Holcomb?"

"Yes."

"Of course I know about it. He told

me . . ." Mason took a cigarette case from his pocket, extended it to Peasley. They both took cigarettes. Mason held a match. "Holcomb's a pretty smart chap," Mason said, casually. "He doesn't miss much."

"I'll tell the world he doesn't."

"How did he find out about the knife, did he tell you?"

"No."

"Did you give him a written statement?"

"Look here," Peasley said, "I'm not supposed to discuss this."

"Oh, Holcomb wouldn't care, if you talked it over with me."

"You're the very one he *didn't* want to know about it."

Mason raised his eyebrows in surprise. "Why, I don't see how that can be, because I *do* know about it."

"Yes, but he didn't think you did."

Mason yawned and said, "Shucks, Peasley, it's all right with me. If you don't want to talk about it, you don't have to."

"Well, I was just following instructions, that was all. You put me in a spot, Mr. Mason."

Mason's face showed surprised incredulity. "I *what?*" he asked.

"Put me in a spot."

"Why, nothing of the sort," Mason said. "You have a right to sell hardware to anyone."

"That isn't the way Sergeant Holcomb looked at it."

"To hell with Sergeant Holcomb," Mason said easily. "Tell him to go jump in the lake. He hasn't got any money invested in the store, has he?"

"No."

"Well, what's bothering you?"

"He said it dragged Helen into it."

"He's a liar," Mason remarked cheerfully. "No one's dragged Helen into anything."

"But I gave you the knife that you were going to substitute for . . ."

"Substitute?" he asked. "For what?"

"Why, for the other knife."

Mason's shake of the head was a slow, solemn gesture of amazed, incredulous negation. "Why, I wasn't going to substitute any knives," he said.

"What did you want it for then?"

"Just to conduct an experiment. In order to perform that experiment, I had to have a knife of the same size and appearance as the one that had killed Rease."

"What was the experiment?"

Mason sucked in a quick breath, as

though about to answer the question in detail, then paused, exhaled and slowly shook his head. "N-n-no, I don't think I'd better tell you. You see, I'm not *quite* ready to confide in Sergeant Holcomb, and he might ask you. It would be a lot better for you to tell him that you didn't know than to tell him that you knew but were sworn to secrecy. Sergeant Holcomb is a bit impulsive at times and he might feel you weren't coöperating with him, particularly if he thinks there's anything questionable about getting that knife for me. I certainly hope he didn't rattle you any, Peasley."

"Well, I was annoyed and a little worried."

"Worried?"

"Yes. Holcomb said something about compounding felonies."

Mason laughed and said, "Don't let a police sergeant tell you what the law is. Get your law from a lawyer. I wouldn't ask you to do anything that wasn't quite all right."

"Well, I'm relieved to hear that. I was worried, not for myself, but for Helen."

"Forget it," Mason told him. "By the way, I want to get some more of those knives."

"Some more of them?"

"Perhaps half a dozen. Do you suppose you could send to the manufacturer and get them?"

"I guess so, yes."

"Would it take a long while?"

"I think I could pick them up from some of the wholesale houses here in town."

"Go ahead and do it, then," Mason instructed, taking a roll of bills from his pocket and tossing a couple of twenties on the counter. "That should cover your expenses as well as compensate you for any extra trouble you go to."

"I'll only charge you the regular price," Peasley said hastily, "but I'd have to get Sergeant Holcomb's permission."

"An attachment on the store?" Mason asked.

"No, certainly not."

"I don't see why you can't sell merchandise without permission from a police officer."

"But he wanted me to keep him advised of anything you said to me. Otherwise, he claimed he'd have to make trouble over that knife business last night."

Mason laughed heartily and said, "Sure, go ahead. Ring him up and tell him I was in and wanted half a dozen more knives. Don't tell him, however, that I've said anything at all about him. He might not like that. Just say I came in and asked you to get me some more knives. If you handle it that way, you won't have to tell him you discussed his visit with me. He's a peculiar chap and he *might* not like it."

"All right," Peasley said with eager alacrity. "I'll do that. I'll handle it just that way, Mr. Mason."

"And, if I see him, I won't mention talking about him with you. That may make it better all around. You can ring him up and tell him I was in asking for half a dozen identical knives. . . . Well, I must be going. Hope I didn't interrupt you."

"Not at all."

"And it won't be too much bother for you to get those half dozen knives?"

"Certainly not."

Mason shook hands and left. At the corner drug store he telephoned his office. "Della there?" he asked.

"No, Mr. Mason, she went out to the hotel you told her to go to. I have the telephone number here."

"Give it to me," Mason said. He made a note of the number, called the Lafitte

Hotel, asked for Miss Street in 609, and shortly afterward heard Della Street's voice on the line. "Holcomb been in the office, Della?" he asked.

"No, why?"

"He pumped Peasley about that knife business."

"He did! What did Peasley tell him?"

"Spilled the whole business."

"How did Sergeant Holcomb know about it in the first place?"

"That's what I'd like to find out."

"Edna Hammer certainly wouldn't have told him."

"One wouldn't think so," Mason agreed.

"Will you be in trouble on account of it, Chief?"

"I don't know. I've done whatever I could to counteract it. That is, I've managed to mix the case all up."

"By doing what?"

"Ordering more of the same article. How are things looking down there?"

"Everything's coming fine."

"Met the woman yet?"

"Yes. Had a nice conversation with her. Very sweet and formal. You know, the nice soft paw covering the sharp claws."

"Swell," he told her. "Met the man yet?"

"No, but I'm going to."

"Stay with it," he said, "I'll give you a ring, if anything new turns up."

—XIX—

THE CLERK SWORE the jury. Judge Markham, shrewd-eyed student of human nature, settled back behind the massive mahogany "bench." Hamilton Burger, the district attorney, broad-shouldered, thick-necked, with the powerful muscles of virile maturity, sat in watchful attention, studying Perry Mason as a catcher observes a runner who is taking a long lead off first base. Beside him sat Sam Blaine, young, tall, slender, and trying to look impressive, fingering the black ribbon which dangled from his glasses. At the opposite counsel table, Perry Mason sat alone. A few feet behind him, Peter Kent, with white, drawn features, kept twisting his fingers. Slightly back of him, Lucille Mays watched proceedings with apprehensive eyes. At times she tried to smile reassuringly at Peter Kent. The effort was a pathetic failure. Judge Markham said, "Permit me to congratulate Counsel for both sides upon the expediency

241

with which jurors have been selected. Do you wish to make an opening speech, Mr. District Attorney?"

District Attorney Burger moved up in front of the bar which separated the twelve curious jurors from the portion of the courtroom reserved for Counsel. Back of the bar, the crowded courtroom was tense with hushed expectancy. Burger said, "Gentlemen, I am not going to indulge in oratory. I shall at this time tell you briefly what the Prosecution expects to prove. On the thirteenth of this month the defendant, Peter Kent, was living in his residence in Hollywood. There were in that residence, besides the servants, Edna Hammer, a niece; P. L. Rease, a half-brother; John J. Duncan, an attorney from Chicago; Frank B. Maddox, a business associate of the defendant; Helen Warrington, the defendant's secretary. We expect to show that on the morning of the fourteenth the defendant entered the bedroom of P. L. Rease and stabbed him to death. We expect to show that P. L. Rease, without the knowledge of the defendant, had exchanged bedrooms with Frank B. Maddox, that between Maddox and the defendant was bad blood; that the defendant labored under the impression, either founded or unfounded, that Maddox was swindling him and trying to hold him up in a business deal.

"As nearly as can be ascertained, the decedent met his death from a stabbing wound inflicted by a carving knife at approximately three o'clock in the morning. Death was instantaneous. We expect to show that at the hour of three o'clock in the morning Peter Kent, the defendant, having this same carving knife in his hand, was moving stealthily, in bare feet, across the patio which separated the wing containing his bedroom from that containing the bedroom of Frank B. Maddox, which was then occupied by the decedent, P. L. Rease. We expect to show that the fatal weapon was subsequently found under the pillow of the bed occupied that night by the defendant; that the blade of the knife shows unmistakably that it was the weapon used to kill P. L. Rease. We expect to show that subsequent to his arrest, the defendant voluntarily admitted that he was an habitual sleepwalker; that he had every reason to believe that while walking in his sleep he had homicidal tendencies.

"The Court will instruct you gentlemen that once the killing by the defendant has been established, the burden of proving circumstances that mitigate, justify or excuse it shifts to the defendant. So far as the Prosecution is concerned, it will show the death of Rease; that the death was due to a stabbing wound inflicted with a carving knife; that the carving knife was in the possession of the defendant at approximately the time of the murder; that the defendant was actually seen leaving the wing of the house containing the bedroom of the decedent at approximately the time of the murder. We expect to show that the defendant thought Maddox occupied the bed in which Rease was sleeping, that the defendant had every motive for murdering Maddox. As you gentlemen have been made aware by questions asked you by the defense when you were selected as jurors, the Defense will rely, at least in part, upon a theory of sleepwalking. We expect to show that upon a prior occasion, approximately one year before the commission of the crime, the defendant secured a carving knife and . . ."

Perry Mason slowly raised himself from his seat and said, "Your Honor, I object to the district attorney incorporating in his statement anything which took place a year before the commission of the crime; object to his seeking to anticipate our defense, and move that the jurors be instructed to disregard his statements."

"The evidence is perfectly proper," Burger retorted, "in that it shows that at a prior time the defendant had knowledge of his homicidal tendencies while walking in his sleep; that he made no effort to curb those tendencies when he realized he was once more walking in his sleep. I am predicating this part of my argument on the theory which the Defense itself has outlined."

Judge Markham rapped with his gavel and said, "It is not incumbent upon the Prosecution to anticipate the Defense. Whether evidence in rebuttal can include incidents taking place prior to the crime and separated from it by a period of twelve months is something which will be determined when the question arises. In the meantime, the objection of the Defense is well taken, the Court will order that that portion of the opening speech be withdrawn from the jury, and the jurors are specifically instructed to disregard it. The jurors are also instructed that the opening statement made by the district attorney merely outlines what he expects to prove and is made for the purpose of clarifying the issues in the minds of the jurors. The statements made by the district attorney are not to be considered as evidence. Go on, Mr. District Attorney."

"We expect to show," Hamilton Burger resumed, "by the defendant's own niece, that prior to the commission of the crime, in fact two days before, she had found the same weapon with which the murder was subsequently committed under the pillow of the defendant's bed. Upon this evidence, Gentlemen, and upon *such other evidence as may be introduced in rebuttal,* the Prosecution will ask at your hands a conviction of first degree murder."

Hamilton Burger sat down. Judge Markham asked Perry Mason, "Do you desire to make an opening statement, Counselor?"

"I will withhold my statement until just before I start to put on *my* case," Mason said.

"Very well, the Prosecution will call its first witness."

"I shall prove the *Corpus Delicti* by calling Frank B. Maddox," Burger said.

Maddox came forward and was sworn.

"Your name is Frank B. Maddox and you reside in Chicago?"

"Yes."

"You were present in the house of the defendant during the night of the thirteenth of this month and the morning of the fourteenth?"

"I was."

"Do you know if P. L. Rease was related to the defendant?"

"He was the defendant's half-brother."

"How long had you been in the defendant's house prior to the thirteenth?"

"I arrived on the tenth."

"On the morning of the fourteenth did you have occasion to see Mr. P. L. Rease?"

"I did."

"Where was he?"

"In his bedroom."

"Was he alive or dead?"

"He was dead, lying in bed flat on his back, with a light blanket drawn up under his chin. There was a cut in the blanket, where a knife had been thrust through the covering and into Mr. Rease's body. The blanket was soaked in blood, and Mr. Rease was dead."

"I shall recall this witness later on," Hamilton Burger said, "for further questions, but at the present time I am merely showing the *Corpus Delicti* and I shall ask permission to withdraw him temporarily."

"Very well," Judge Markham said.

"Do you wish to cross-examine?" Burger inquired.

"Yes," Mason said. "You say you were in the house during the evening of the thirteenth, Mr. Maddox?"

"Yes."

"When did you first leave the house on the morning of the fourteenth?"

"Is that material?" Burger asked, frowning.

"I think so."

"I don't. I object to it on the ground that it is immaterial, that it is not proper cross-examination."

Judge Markham hesitated a moment. "I will," Perry Mason said, "amend the question, to make it as follows: When did you first leave the house on the morning of the fourteenth *prior to the time the body was discovered?*"

"That question is plainly within the scope of cross-examination," Judge Markham ruled. "Answer it."

"I didn't leave the house at all," Maddox said.

Mason raised his eyebrows. "Didn't you leave the house about three o'clock in the morning?" he asked.

"No."

"You went to your room the evening of the thirteenth at what time?"

"Approximately nine-thirty I should judge."

"Did you go to bed immediately after going to your room?"

"No, my attorney, Mr. Duncan, went to my room with me. We were engaged in a long conference."

"What time did you arise on the morning of the fourteenth?" Mason asked.

"I was aroused by you and Dr. Kelton invading my room, trying to find out who had been killed. . . ."

"Move to strike out that portion of the answer as a conclusion of the witness," Mason said.

"It will go out," Judge Markham ruled. "The jury will disregard it."

"What time was it?"

"Around eight o'clock, I think."

"And you wish the jury to understand, Mr. Maddox, that you were continuously in the house from the time you retired on the evening of the thirteenth to eight o'clock in the morning of the fourteenth?"

"Yes, sir."

"Didn't you go to the Pacific Greyhound Stage Depot at approximately three o'clock in the morning on the fourteenth and place a long distance call for Mrs. Doris Sully Kent in Santa Barbara?"

Maddox clamped his lips tightly together and shook his head. "You'll have to answer the question audibly," the court reporter announced.

"I most certainly did not," Maddox said, speaking distinctly.

"You didn't?" Mason asked, surprise in his voice.

"No, sir."

"Were you up at approximately three o'clock in the morning?"

"I wasn't even awake."

"Didn't you," Mason asked, "engage in a conference with Mr. Duncan, your attorney, some time around three o'clock in the morning of the fourteenth?"

"No, sir, absolutely not."

"At any time between midnight of the thirteenth and five o'clock in the morning of the fourteenth?"

"Absolutely not."

Mason said, "That's all."

Hamilton Burger called a draftsman who produced plans of the Kent residence. The plans were offered in evidence and received without objection. The coroner fixed the time of death as some time between two-thirty and three-thirty on the morning of the fourteenth. Detective Sergeant Holcomb took the witness stand and identified the carving knife, with its blade stained a sinister, rusty red, as the weapon which had been found under the pillow of Kent's bed. Perry Mason, who had not cross-examined the other witnesses, asked Sergeant Holcomb, "What happened to the pillowcase and the sheets on that bed?"

"I don't know."

"You don't know?"

"Well, I was told that they had been put in the laundry by the housekeeper."

"She didn't save them?"

"No."

"Why didn't you produce them as evidence?"

"Because I didn't think I needed to."

"Isn't it a fact that there were no blood stains whatever on the pillow or on the sheet?"

"I don't think so. I think there were blood stains, but I can't remember."

Mason said sneeringly, "If there *had* been blood stains you'd have thought the articles of sufficient importance to impound them as evidence, wouldn't you?"

"Objected to as argumentative," Burger stormed.

"Merely for the purpose of refreshing the witness's recollection," Mason said. "He has testified that he doesn't know whether there were any blood stains."

"Let him answer the question," Judge Markham ruled.

"I don't know," Sergeant Holcomb admitted, and then added, "You should know, Mr. Mason. *You* were the one who discovered the carving knife."

Spectators in the courtroom tittered. Perry Mason said, "Yes, *I* know. Are you asking *me* to tell *you*, Sergeant?"

Judge Markham pounded his gavel. "That will do," he ordered. "The witness will be interrogated by proper questions. There will be no more exchanges between the witness and counsel."

"And," Mason charged, raising his voice, "since the sheet and pillowcase were free of blood stains and might, therefore, be evidence which would militate against the theory of the Prosecution, you saw to it that these articles found their way into the laundry while *you* were in exclusive charge of the premises, and before the Defense had a chance to preserve them, didn't you?"

With a roar, Burger was on his feet, objecting, ". . . argumentative, improper, no proper foundation laid, insulting, not proper cross-examination, incompetent, irrelevant and immaterial." Perry Mason merely smiled.

"The witness may answer," Judge Markham ruled. "As asked, the question goes to the bias or interest of the witness."

"No," Sergeant Holcomb said, "I didn't have anything to do with the sheets."

"But you did suggest to the housekeeper she had better clean up the room?"

"Perhaps I did."

"And make the bed?"

"Perhaps."

"That," Mason announced with a triumphant glance at the jury, "is all."

"Call John J. Duncan," Blaine announced as Hamilton Burger settled back in his chair, to let his deputy take the lead for a while. Duncan strutted pompously forward and was sworn. "Your name is John

J. Duncan. You are an attorney from Illinois, and you know the defendant, Peter Kent?"

"Yes."

"You were, I believe, in his house on the thirteenth and the morning of the fourteenth of this month?"

"That's right. I engaged in a business conference with Mr. Kent and with Mr. Perry Mason, his attorney. There were also present at the conference Helen Warrington, Mr. Kent's secretary, and my client, Frank B. Maddox. I believe there was also present a Dr. Kelton."

"What time did you retire?"

"Around eleven o'clock. I had a talk with my client in his bedroom after the meeting with these other gentlemen split up."

"Did you see Mr. Kent later on during the evening?"

"I saw him early on the morning of the fourteenth."

"At what time?"

"At precisely three o'clock in the morning."

"*Where* did you see him?"

"In the patio of the house."

"Can you point out on the map, People's Exhibit Number One, the exact spot where you first saw the defendant at that time?" Duncan indicated a point on the diagram. "And where on the diagram is your bedroom located?" Duncan indicated. "And from your bedroom you could plainly see the defendant?"

"Yes, sir."

"When did you first see him?"

"I was awakened by a shadow falling across my face. I woke up and saw someone moving across the porch. I jumped up, looked at the clock to see what time it was, and went to the window. I saw Peter Kent, the defendant, attired only in a nightgown, walking across the patio. He had a knife in his hand. He walked to a coffee table, paused for a few moments and then crossed the patio and vanished through the door on the other side."

"By 'the door on the other side' you mean the spot which I am now indicating on the map, People's Exhibit Number One, and marked for identification 'Door on North Side of Patio'?"

"I do."

"And approximately where was this coffee table located?" Duncan made a mark with a crayon on the map.

"You say you looked at the clock?"

"I did."

"And what time was it?"

"Three o'clock."

"Did you turn on a light to see the clock?"

"I did not. The clock had a luminous dial and I was able to see the position of the hands."

"Did you look at the clock before or after you observed the figure in the patio?"

"Both. I looked at it as soon as I sat up in bed, and I looked at it when I returned to bed after seeing the defendant cross the patio and vanish through that door."

"What did you do, if anything?"

"I was very much concerned, put on a bathrobe, opened the door from my bedroom into the corridor, looked up and down the corridor, saw no one and then decided that, since I was in a hostile house, I'd mind my own business. I went back to bed and eventually went to sleep."

"I think, if the court please," Mason said, "we are entitled to have stricken from the answer of the witness the fact that he was in a hostile house. That is a conclusion of the witness and the answer, insofar as it relates to his motives, is not responsive to the question, and is, in addition, objectionable."

"It may be stricken out," Judge Markham ruled.

Blaine turned to Perry Mason and said, "You may cross-examine, Mr. Mason. Perhaps *you'll* want to ask him why he went back to his sleep."

Judge Markham frowned at Blaine and said, "That will do, Mr. Blaine."

"Yes," Mason said easily, "I will ask him just that. Mr. Duncan, how did it happen that you were able to go back to bed and go to sleep after seeing so startling a sight?"

Duncan leaned forward impressively. "Because I was tired," he said. "I'd been listening to you talk all the evening."

The courtroom burst into a roar of laughter. The bailiff pounded with his gavel. Judge Markham waited until order had been restored, then said to the witness, "Mr. Duncan, you're an attorney. You need no instructions as to the duties of a witness. You will please refrain from attempting to provoke laughter or from adding to your answers comments which are uncalled for. You will also refrain from indulging in personalities with counsel."

Duncan hesitated a moment, then said, in a surly manner, "Yes, Your Honor.

Judge Markham stared steadily at the witness, seemed about to add something to his admonition, but slowly settled back in his chair, nodded to Mason and said, "Proceed, Counselor."

"If the Court please," Mason said, "I am perfectly willing to take the answer of the witness at its face value. I am not asking to have any part of it stricken out. I would like to cross-examine him upon that statement."

"Very well," Judge Markham said, "you may cross-examine him on that statement just as much as you want to, Counselor."

Mason rose to his feet, stared steadily at Duncan. "So you were so tired from hearing me talk all evening that you were able to go back to sleep, is that right?"

"That's what I said."

"You talked with your client for an hour or so after you both sought your rooms?"

"Yes."

"My talk hadn't made you so sleepy that you couldn't stay awake to discuss certain matters of strategy with your client?"

"I talked with him."

"And went to bed about eleven o'clock?"

"Yes."

"Yet, after four hours of sleep, the soothing effect of my conversation was still so great that the startling apparition of a man clad only in a nightdress, carrying a carving knife and prowling around in the moonlight didn't interfere with your slumbers, is that right?"

"I was awakened. I looked up and down the corridor," Duncan said.

Mason continued to bore in. "And went back to sleep, Mr. Duncan?"

"I went back to sleep."

"Within a very few minutes?"

"Within a very few minutes."

"And you have testified on oath that you were able to do this because of the wearying effect of my conversation?"

"You know what I meant."

"The only means I have of knowing what you meant, Mr. Duncan, is what you said, and that, of course, is the only way that the jury has of knowing what you meant. Now, let's be frank with the jury. *I* didn't talk at our conference more than a very few minutes, did I?"

"I didn't time you."

"For the most part my conversation consisted in saying 'No' to your demands, didn't it?"

"I don't think we need to go into that."

"But when you said my talk had made you so tired that you had no difficulty in going back to sleep you were exaggerating the facts of the case, weren't you?"

"I went back to sleep."

"Yes, Mr. Duncan, and the real reason you went back to sleep is because you didn't see anything particularly alarming about the figure when you first noticed it, isn't that right?"

"A man walking around at night with a carving knife is alarming to me," Duncan snapped. "I don't know whether it would alarm you or not."

"Exactly," Mason said. "And *if* you had seen a carving knife in the hand of the person you saw walking about the patio at three o'clock in the morning of the fourteenth, you would have been sufficiently startled to have notified the police or aroused the household, wouldn't you?"

"I don't understand your question. I saw the figure, I saw the knife and I went back to sleep."

"I'll get at it another way," Mason said.

"Isn't it a fact that you *didn't* see the carving knife clearly?"

"No, I saw it."

"This same carving knife?" Mason asked, gesturing toward the blood-stained knife which had been introduced in evidence.

"That same one," Duncan snapped. Mason said nothing but stood smiling at him. Duncan fidgeted uncomfortably and said, "At any rate, a knife which looked very much like that."

Mason stepped back to the counsel table, opened his brief case and pulled out a brown paper parcel, took off the paper and produced a horn-handled carving knife. "I will hand you this carving knife," he said to the witness, "and ask you if *this* isn't the carving knife which was in the hand of the figure which you saw walking across the patio."

Duncan said savagely, "No, it isn't."

"How do you know it isn't?" Mason asked.

"Well," Duncan said, "I don't think it's the same one."

"You want the Court and the jury to understand that you could see that carving knife plainly enough to identify it?"

"Not to identify it, but I could get a general description of it."

"And you're certain this wasn't the carving knife?"

"I don't think it was."

"Are you certain it wasn't?"

"Well, of course, I couldn't be certain at that distance."

"Then you can't be certain that this knife, which has been introduced by the People as Exhibit Number Two, *was* the same knife, can you?"

"Well, no," Duncan said, "I can't."

"I think," Mason remarked, "I'm going to ask the Court to have this second knife marked for identification as defendant's Exhibit A."

"I object," Burger shouted. "That knife, Your Honor, doesn't enter into the case in any way. That is simply a trick by which the counsel for the Defense has sought to becloud the issue. I can prove that counsel for the Defense got that knife long after the murder through a hardware . . ."

Mason whirled savagely toward him, but before he could interrupt, Judge Markham had snapped forth a ruling. "That will do, Mr. District Attorney. Never mind what you can prove as to the source of the knife. This witness has testified that the figure he saw in the patio was carrying a knife which he thinks was People's Exhibit Number Two; that it was, at any rate, similar in appearance. It is legitimate cross-examination to produce another knife and ask him the questions which Counselor Mason has asked. No objection was made to those questions when they were put to the witness. Counselor is now asking only that the knife be marked for identification, in order that the identical knife concerning which the witness was interrogated can be identified. It is entirely proper. The Court will mark the knife for identification as defendant's Exhibit A."

Mason turned, suddenly whirled to face Duncan and said, "Mr. Duncan, isn't the real reason that you were able to go back to sleep due to the fact you didn't realize at the time the figure you saw was carrying a knife?"

"I saw that he was carrying something in his hand, something that glittered."

"But isn't it a fact that you didn't realize that it was a knife and it wasn't until after the murder had been discovered the next morning that it occurred to you that it must have been a knife? Didn't you see merely a white figure walking in his sleep; and didn't you decide that you weren't going to interfere, but safeguarded yourself against intrusion by locking your door, and then went back to sleep?"

"I didn't say the man was walking in his sleep."

"But I'm asking you if it isn't a fact."

"No."

"And isn't it true that the only reason you were able to go back to sleep was because you didn't see a knife in his hand clearly enough to recognize what the object was?"

"No, I don't think so."

"Can you be more positive than that?"

"Yes. I saw the knife."

"Now, the figure went to the coffee table in the patio?"

"Yes."

"Did you see him raise the lid of the coffee table?"

"Yes."

"And you saw the figure then leave the coffee table, walk across the patio and leave the patio by the door which you have indicated?"

"Yes."

"After the figure left the table, did it continue to carry the knife?"

"Why, yes . . . I don't . . . I can't say."

"Would you say that it was *not* carrying the knife?"

"I wouldn't say one way or another."

"Then it is possible that the figure left the knife in the oblong receptacle underneath the top of the coffee table?"

"I can't say."

"Are you certain that the figure had a knife *before* it reached the coffee table?"

"Objected to, as already asked and answered a dozen different times," Burger said.

"I'll let him answer this one question," Judge Markham ruled, leaning forward and staring steadily at Duncan.

"Yes," Duncan said, "he had a knife in his hand."

"You're certain of the identity of the figure you saw?" Mason asked.

"I am."

"It was the defendant?"

"It was."

"How was he dressed?"

"Only in a night shirt."

"His feet were bare?"

"Yes."

"How close was he to you when you first saw him distinctly?"

"He crossed in front of my window."

"And threw a shadow on your face?"

"Yes."

"But at that time you couldn't see him distinctly. You were in bed and you wakened from a sound sleep, is that right?"

"Yes."

"How far away was he when you first saw him clearly?"

"I can't tell you exactly."

"Can you point out on the map?"

"Yes, he was approximately here."

Mason marked the spot with a crayon, then, by referring to the scale of the map, said, "In other words, he was approximately thirty-five feet away?"

"It may have been that, yes."

"His back was to you?"

"Yes, I believe it was."

"And yet you recognized him?"

"I recognized him."

"You understand the importance of being absolutely correct in your testimony?"

"I do."

"Certainly."

"And yet you are willing to swear positively that this figure which you saw, wear-

266

ing only a nightgown, a figure walking away from you, at a distance of thirty-five feet, in the moonlight, was the defendant?"

"I do."

"You looked at the clock when you got up?"

"Yes."

"And again when you came back to bed?"

"I think so, yes."

"What time was it when you first got up?"

"Exactly three o'clock."

"What time was it when you came back to bed?"

"Why, just about the same time, I don't suppose over thirty seconds had elapsed."

"And you noticed the hands of the clock for the second time, just before you got in bed?"

"Yes."

"As a matter of fact, wasn't it quarter past twelve?"

"No."

"When you first reported what you had seen, didn't you place the time at quarter past twelve?"

"I may have."

"At that time, your recollections were

more vivid and fresh than they are now, were they not?"

"No."

"They weren't?"

"No."

"Do I understand you to say that your recollection becomes more vivid with the passage of time?"

"It does in this case, yes."

"Because when you learned the killing must have taken place at approximately three o'clock you transposed the position of the hands of the clock in your mind so that you could be a star witness in this case and . . ."

Judge Markham pounded with his gavel. "I think, Counselor, that about the star witness is unnecessary."

"I wish to show the motive of the witness."

"It isn't so!" Duncan shouted. "I *know* now that it was three o'clock in the morning. There's no chance it was quarter past twelve."

"Your eyesight's good?" Mason asked.

"Very good!"

"And it was on the morning of the fourteenth?"

"Certainly."

"You wore glasses, didn't you?"

"I have worn glasses for thirty-five years."

"And you were wearing glasses habitually during the period covered in your testimony?"

"Yes."

"Did you put on your glasses when you got up to look out of the window?"

"No. . . . Yes, I guess I did. I think I must have."

"Why did you put them on?"

"To see with, of course."

Once more there was a titter which ran around the courtroom, but this time, something in the tense attitude of Perry Mason caused the titter to subside even before the bailiff could rap for order. "In other words, then," Mason said, "when you were aroused by a marauder prowling about your room in the dead of night, the very first thing you did after wakening was to put on your glasses so that you could see to better advantage, is that right?"

"Well, what's wrong with that?"

"Nothing is wrong with it, Mr. Duncan, I am asking you if that is what happened."

"Yes, I guess so."

"In other words, you knew that your eyes

would be virtually valueless without the glasses."

"I didn't say that."

"No," Mason said, smiling, *"you* didn't say it, but your actions said it more plainly than words. You put on your glasses because you knew you couldn't see without them. Isn't that right?"

"I knew they'd help me to see."

"You knew that you couldn't see clearly any great distance without them, didn't you?"

"Well, my eyesight's a lot better with them on than with them off."

"And with your glasses your eyesight was quite good?" Mason asked.

"Oh, yes."

"Would you say it was perfect?"

"I'd say that it was normal."

"Perfectly normal?"

"If you want to express it that way, yes."

"Then," Mason said, pointing his forefinger at Duncan, "why was it that, immediately after you had reported to the district attorney what you had seen, you were sent to an oculist *to have new glasses fitted?"*

Burger shouted, "He wasn't instructed

to do any such thing! I resent that insinuation!"

"Why did you do it?" Mason asked Duncan.

"I didn't say that I did it."

Mason, pounding his fist on the counsel table, said, "*I* say you did it, then. *Why* did you do it?"

Duncan squirmed uncomfortably. "Well," he said, "I wanted to, that's all."

"Why did you want to?"

"I'd been wanting to for some time and hadn't had a chance to do it. I'd been too busy. You understand I'm a very busy attorney."

"Oh," Mason said, "you'd been putting it off, then, for some time."

"Yes."

"You're quite busy?"

"Yes."

"How long have you been quite busy?"

"For years."

"And did you put off getting these glasses during the time you'd been busy?"

"During much of it, yes."

"You'd put off getting these glasses for years, then, is that right?"

"Yes. . . . No, that isn't what I meant."

"Never mind what you meant. What are

the facts of the case? How long had you put off getting new glasses?"

"I don't know.

"When were you last fitted for glasses before the fourteenth of this month?"

"I can't tell you that."

"As much as five years ago?"

"I don't know."

"As much as ten years ago?"

"I don't think so."

"And the very first thing you did after telling the district attorney what you saw was to go out and consult an oculist and get glasses. Isn't that right?"

"It wasn't the first thing I did."

"It was just about the first thing you did, wasn't it?"

"I don't know."

"It was that evening, wasn't it?"

"Yes, it was that evening."

"And did you find an oculist in his office on that evening?"

"Yes."

Mason's smile was fiendish. "You found him there, Mr. Duncan, because you had previously telephoned and made an appointment with him, isn't that right?"

Duncan hesitated a minute and then said, "No, I didn't telephone to him."

Mason frowned for a moment, then triumphantly asked, "Who *did* telephone to him?"

Blaine jumped to his feet. "Your Honor," he said, "that's objected to as incompetent, irrelevant and immaterial. It makes no difference who telephoned to the oculist."

"It does, in view of the answers the witness has been giving to these questions," Perry Mason said. "This is a witness who is an attorney. I have a right to impeach his testimony by showing the condition of his eyesight at the time in question. This witness has admitted that he needed glasses and has also admitted that the glasses he put on were insufficient and had been insufficient for years. I also have a right to show his bias and interest, as developed by his evasive answers."

"I think," Judge Markham said, "I'll permit him to answer the question. Who telephoned the oculist, Mr. Duncan, if you know?" Duncan hesitated.

"Go on," Mason said, "answer the question."

In a voice which was barely audible, Duncan said, "Mr. Blaine."

"The deputy district attorney," Mason inquired, "who has just finished making such a vociferous objection that my question was incompetent, irrelevant and immaterial?"

A roar of laughter swept the courtroom. Judge Markham frowned, then permitted himself a half-smile. "That will do, Counselor," he said sternly, then, looking at the clock, "It has approached the hour of adjournment. I think we have made very good progress for today. Court will adjourn until tomorrow. The Court is going to remand the jury to the custody of the sheriff, who will keep them in his charge and permit no person to approach them or address them, nor will he address them himself, except upon matters not connected in any way with the case. Court is adjourned until ten o'clock tomorrow morning."

—XX—

MASON, PACING BACK and forth across his office, looked frowningly at Della Street. The indirect lights failed to soften the scowl lines which were furrowed across the lawyer's forehead. "Damn it, Della," he said, "the thing doesn't click."

"Why doesn't it click?"

"I can't understand what's wrong with Mrs. Kent."

"You haven't heard anything from her?"

"Not a thing. You're certain that Pritchard met her?"

"Absolutely. He was making a rush play for me, but he dropped me like a hot potato when I told him about Mrs. Kent's money."

"Good looking?"

"I'll say."

"Make your heart go pitty-pat?" he asked.

"Not mine, but he's a swell looker. He looks like a Venus de Hollywood."

"Hair?"

"Wonderful, dark rich brown, beautifully marcelled. Lights in it. And they match his eyes. Boyish face, without a line in it. A little trick mustache. He wears his clothes nicely and his lips are fascinating, particularly when he talks. You can see them forming every word so distinctly. And when he dances, he makes you feel like thistle-down."

"She seemed to be falling?"

"Falling is right. She was looking at him with her heart in her eyes."

"How the devil can a woman get her heart in her eyes?"

"Want me to show you?" she challenged. He took a quick step toward her. Her eyes studied his face appraisingly, "Strictly for the sake of the business?" she added.

His arm was reaching for her when knuckles made a gentle tapping motion on the corridor door. Mason froze into rigid immobility. The knock was repeated. "Bet you five bucks *that's* Doris Sully Kent," he said.

Della Street started for the law library. "I knew *something* would happen," she remarked, jerking the door open "Be sure to switch on the loud speaker, Chief. I've got pencils and notebook in there." She closed the door behind her with a slam.

Mason stepped to the corridor door. Doris Sully Kent smiled up at him. "I knew I'd find you here, Mr. Mason."

"Come in," he invited.

She entered the room, smiled sweetly at him, placed herself in a chair so that her blonde hair showed to advantage against the black leather. "Working hard?" she asked.

"Yes."

"I'm sorry I interrupted you, but I thought you might be interested."

"You have a lawyer?"

"Not me. Not now."

"Well?" he asked.

She extended a gloved forefinger and traced little curving lines along the skirt where it was stretched tightly over her leg. Her eyes followed the moving tip of her forefinger. While she spoke she did not once glance at him. "I've been thinking things over. I'm willing to admit I started that Santa Barbara action because I knew Pete was going to get married again, and I didn't see any reason why I should let him dissipate his property on some gold-digger. I understand the woman is a nurse. Think of it, Peter Kent marrying a nurse!"

"What's wrong with a nurse?" Mason asked.

"Everything," she replied, "so far as Peter Kent is concerned. She has to work for a living."

"And a mighty fine thing," Mason said. "I like women who work for a living."

"It isn't that. It's not that I'm snobbish. It's the fact that she's after Peter Kent's money."

"I don't agree with you."

"We don't need to discuss it, do we?"

"*You* brought it up."

"Well, I was just trying to explain to you why I had a change of heart."

"Do I understand you're trying to tell me you've experienced a change of heart?"

"Yes."

"Why?"

"I suddenly decided that, even if Peter is a little off mentally, and wants to squander his money, I shouldn't stop him. If that's what it takes to make him happy, I want him to be happy."

"So what?" Mason asked skeptically.

"I knew you wouldn't believe me," she said wearily, "you think I'm cold-blooded and mercenary. I do wish I could do something to convince you I wasn't. I value your good opinion very much indeed, Mr. Mason, more, perhaps, than you realize. I have met lots of attorneys, but I have never met anyone who seemed to be as straightforward, as vigorous, and as . . . as ruggedly honest as you are. And I could see you didn't like me. Men usually like me. I want very much to have you like me."

Mason opened his cigarette case, extended it to her. She took a cigarette, suddenly lifted her eyes to his, smiled and said, "Say 'thank you.'"

"Thank you," Mason said, tonelessly. He gave her a light, then transferred the flaming match to the tip of his own cigarette and regarded her quizzically through a cloud of cigarette smoke. "Well?"

"The district attorney wants to put me on the witness stand."

"To prove what?"

"To prove that Peter tried to kill me with a carving knife."

"Does he think he can use your testimony?"

"He said, to use his exact words, 'Somewhere along the line Mason will open the door so I can use you on rebuttal.'"

"Anything else?"

"You're not making it particularly easy for me."

"If I knew just what you had in mind," he told her, "I might make it easier."

"I want to let Peter have his divorce."

"Why?"

"Because I think that's the best thing for him."

"And just how do you propose to go about it?" he asked.

"I want to dismiss all of my actions. That would clear everything up. The final decree has already been granted, and, if I dismiss everything, that would give Peter a clean slate, wouldn't it?"

Mason didn't answer her question directly but said, "Just how much did you expect in return?"

"What made you think I expected anything?"

"Don't you?"

"I'm not mercenary. I don't want any of Peter's money, but I'm untrained, I haven't any profession, I haven't any skill nor any calling. I can't even run a typewriter or take shorthand."

"How much?" he asked.

Some swift emotion flamed in her eyes, then died. "How much would *you* suggest?" she asked, demurely.

"I couldn't make any suggestion."

"You could suggest what Peter would be willing to pay, couldn't you?"

"No."

"I'd take two hundred thousand dollars in cash. That would enable me to keep on living in the style to which Peter accustomed me."

"Don't do it," Mason told her; "it isn't worth it."

"Isn't worth what?"

"Going on living at that price."

"You're trying to tell me how I should live?" she flared.

He shook his head and said, "No, I'm trying to tell you what you can't get."

"What can't I get?"

"Two hundred thousand dollars."

"I don't see," she told him, her finger now making rapid excursions over the dress material, "how I could get along on any less."

"Oh, well," Mason said, "you're getting fifteen hundred a month. Suppose you go ahead and keep on taking that. That would be a lot better than a lump sum. You'll have a fixed monthly income and, if anything should happen, you'd be taken care of."

"How long would that continue?"

"Indefinitely," he told her, "unless, of course, you got married."

"No," she said, "I don't want to be a drain on Peter that way. I would prefer just taking some little settlement and getting out."

"What do you mean by a little settlement?"

"Two hundred thousand dollars."

Mason shook his head gravely. "No, I wouldn't suggest that my client pay you a lump sum. You've been so fair all the way through that I really think you'd better keep that fifteen hundred a month. I'd say that, in the long run, you'd be a lot better off than if you had a large sum of money."

"Suppose I came down?"

"How much?"

"Suppose I told you exactly what my lowest price is, Mr. Mason? One hundred thousand dollars." Mason yawned, covered the yawn with polite fingers, shook his head. "You're *very* difficult to deal with."

"Oh, well," Mason told her, "go ahead and get an attorney, if you feel that way about it, and I'll deal through him."

"I don't want to split with any lawyer." Mason shrugged his shoulders. She suddenly dashed her cigarette to the floor, jumped to her feet and said, "Well, make me an offer! Don't sit there like a bump on a log. I've got things to do."

"What?" he asked her, raising his eyebrows.

"None of your damn business. Make me an offer."

"For what?"

"For a complete clean-up all the way along the line."

"You'll get out?"

"I'll say I'll get out."

"Without bothering Peter Kent or seeing him again?"

"If I *never* see him again, that's six months too soon."

Mason shook his head and said slowly, "No, I think my client has changed his mind about getting married. Only yesterday he mentioned how beautiful you were. Frankly I think it might be possible to effect a reconciliation."

"I don't want a reconciliation." Mason shrugged his shoulders. "Look here," she said, still standing, her eyes glittering, cheeks flushed. "I read the newspaper accounts of the trial today."

"Well?" he asked.

"Well, Maddox was asked about a telephone call."

"Well?"

"Suppose you could prove he was lying?"

"That," Mason said, "would be most advantageous."

"Well, suppose I got on the witness stand and admitted receiving a telephone call from him. What would that be worth to you?"

"Not a damn cent," Mason said. "We're

not going to buy perjured testimony from anyone."

"But suppose it was the truth?"

"*Is* it the truth?"

"I'm not going to answer the question just yet."

"When you get on the witness stand," Mason said, "you'll answer the question."

"And I'll answer it any way I damn please," she told him, coming over to the corner of the desk and pounding it with her fist. "Don't think you're going to bully me, Mr. Perry Mason."

"You don't mean you'd commit perjury, do you?"

"Certainly I'd commit perjury! Men make me sick. They lie to women up one side and down the other and, if a woman lies back, they think she's deceitful. . . . Give me fifty thousand!"

Mason shook his head. She clenched her fists. "I'd recommend twenty-five thousand to my client," Mason said slowly.

"He'd pay it, if you recommended it."

"I'd recommend it, if you'd tell the absolute truth."

"A bargain?" she asked. He nodded. "Damn you," she told him, "I hate you! If Pete hadn't been in jail over this thing,

I could have gone to him and got two hundred thousand as easy as not. Perhaps more."

"Go ahead and hate me," Mason said, smiling.

"I do," she told him, "but, if I ever get into a jam, you're going to be my lawyer."

"Meaning you're thinking of shooting a husband some day?" he asked.

Slowly the anger died in her eyes. She perched herself on the arm of the big overstuffed leather chair and said, "Don't be silly, do I look like a fool? I should kill the geese that lay the golden eggs."

"All right," Mason said, "I'll get you twenty-five thousand dollars."

"When?"

"Tomorrow morning. The check to be delivered to you before you go on the witness stand so there won't be any question about a pending settlement between you and your husband when you testify."

"Make it thirty thousand."

"Twenty-five," he said with finality. She sighed. "What about your conversations with Maddox?" he asked.

"You want the whole story?"

"Yes."

"Duncan got in touch with me first. He

said he was Maddox's lawyer. He called me around eleven o'clock and said he wanted a conference and suggested they meet in my lawyer's office. Then at three o'clock in the morning Maddox telephoned and I explained to him that I'd already discussed the matter with his lawyer."

"Did you have the conference?"

"Yes."

"What did they suggest?"

"They must have thought I was a fool. They wanted me to sign a *written* agreement that they'd help me have Pete declared incompetent and that then I was going to make a complete release of all of Pete's rights in the Maddox Manufacturing Company and give them one hundred thousand dollars in cash as soon as I got control of Pete's property."

"What did you tell them?"

"I told them I'd have to think it over."

"Did you say how long you were going to take thinking it over?"

"No."

"Did they try to rush you?"

"Of course."

"Can you tell exactly when Duncan called you?"

"No, it was some time around eleven o'clock, between ten and eleven."

"Exactly when Maddox called you?"

"That was three o'clock in the morning. I looked at my watch. It made me so damn mad to be wakened at that hour, because I couldn't get back to sleep."

Mason took some typewritten notes from his desk. "Did you," he asked, "say over the telephone, in answer to Maddox's call, words to this effect?" and Mason read slowly from his notes, "'Hello. . . . yes, this is Mrs. Kent. . . . Yes, Mrs. Doris Sully Kent of Santa Barbara. . . . What's that name again, please?. . . Maddox. . . . I don't understand your calling at this hour. . . . Why, I thought that was all fixed. Your lawyer has arranged a conference, and I'll meet you, as agreed . . . You can get in touch with Mr. Sam Hettley, of the firm of Hettley and Hettley, if you want any more information. Goodby.'"

"Why, yes?" she exclaimed. "Those must have been my exact words! How did you know?"

Mason shook his head, went on with his questioning. "Then what did you do?"

"Tried to sleep for an hour or so and

then got in my car and drove to Los Angeles."

"Where was your car?"

"It happened that it was in a neighbor's garage, about half a block down the street."

"Did you make any attempt to sneak out of your house?"

She shook her head. "Not consciously. There'd been someone hanging around in front of the house. I thought perhaps Peter had decided to put a detective on me, which would have been foolish because I'd never have left a back trail *he* could have followed. I've had detectives on my trail before."

"So you tried to sneak out?"

"Well, I didn't go out with a brass band."

"Went out the back door?"

"Yes."

"And along the cement walk?"

"No, I kept to the grassy stretch on the side."

"So your feet wouldn't make any noise?"

"Yes."

"And you weren't followed when you came to Los Angeles?"

"No, but I met a man in the hallway of the office building where my lawyer has his office, who looked like a detective. I was a little bit frightened. I told my lawyer to be careful and fix things so Maddox and Duncan didn't leave the office for an hour after I left."

"One more question," Mason said. "Where were you on the thirteenth?"

"The day before the murder?"

"Yes."

"In Los Angeles."

"Doing what?"

"Shopping and consulting with my lawyers."

"Anything else?"

She thought a minute, then laughed and said, "I saw Pete on the street and followed him for a while."

"Why?"

"I don't know—just curiosity, I guess. I followed him here and knew he'd been consulting with you. I'd fired my Santa Barbara lawyers, and when I saw Pete come here I knew things were coming to a head, so then was when I went to see Hettley."

"How far did you follow Mr. Kent?"

"Until he started for Hollywood. I thought some of stopping him and talking settlement. I wish I'd done it now."

"That," Mason said, "is better. Inasmuch as your appearance in court has been made through Hettley and Hettley, you'll have to have them sign the releases. You get those releases and I'll have a check for twenty-five thousand dollars all ready for you."

"That's okay," she said, "I made Hettley and Hettley sign the request for dismissal and all of that a couple of days ago. I have all of the necessary papers with me."

"How did you get them to do that?"

"Do we have to go into that?" she asked.

"I'd like to get a complete picture of the situation."

"It was simple," she told him, her lips curving in a smile. "I told them that I'd made some perjured allegations in my complaint and asked them if they wanted to go ahead with the case in view of that fact. I told them that I'd made some very damaging admissions to a very attractive young woman who, it turned out, was a detective, and the other side knew of my perjury. Naturally, they were so anxious to get out they told me never to darken their doors again. I paid them five hundred dollars for drawing up the papers and they washed their hands of the entire case."

"Do you always play both ends against the middle?" he asked her.

"Sure. I'm attractive. Men never married

me for love—not the kind I married. They were old buzzards with money. . . . If I ever marry again, it'll be for love. I'm tired of gold-digging."

"Thinking of getting married?" he asked her.

"No, of course not."

"Very well," he told her, "I'll have your money in the morning."

He escorted her to the door. She turned in the corridor and said, "You won't tell Hettley and Hettley about the trick I've pulled on them, will you?"

"Not me," Mason told her. "All I want is to have the releases and dismissals in proper form and you'll get your twenty-five thousand dollars. You'll also be subpoenaed as a witness for the defense."

"Swell," she told him.

"And don't make the mistake of trying to change your story after I get you on the stand," he told her.

"Don't worry," she said, "I know enough about men to know when I'm monkeying with a buzz saw. I'll play ball with you, Mr. Mason."

He bowed, smiled and closed the door. Della Street emerged from the law library, carrying a notebook and pencils. "The damn little double-crosser," she said. "I could snatch her hair out. What a little tramp she is!"

Mason chuckled and said, "Anyone who can slip one over on Hettley and Hettley is entitled to it. It was a case of diamond cut diamond. They thought they were going to stick her plenty. She just beat them to it."

"I hated to see you give her twenty-five thousand dollars," Della Street said. "I'll bet she'd have dismissed her case anyway. She's crazy over Pritchard."

"Don't worry," Mason told her; "your friend, George Pritchard will get most of it. And he needs the money to pay off Myrna Duchene. You might get Myrna on the telephone and suggest that now would be a good time to drop into Pritchard's hotel and threaten to have him arrested unless he kicks through with the money by tomorrow morning."

Della Street reached for the telephone. "And will *that* give me pleasure," she exclaimed.

—XXI—

JUDGE MARKHAM, SETTLING himself in the massive swivel chair behind the bench, glanced at the jury box and said, "May it be stipulated, gentlemen, that the jurors are all present and the defendant is in court?"

"So stipulated," Mason said.

"And so stipulated for the Prosecution," Hamilton Burger announced.

"I believe Mr. Duncan was on the stand for further cross-examination," Judge Markham said. "Come forward, Mr. Duncan."

Duncan strutted to the witness stand, his manner radiating importance. "I think I have just one more question," Mason said, when the witness had taken his seat. "I believe you stated, Mr. Duncan, that you talked with your client, Mr. Maddox, until approximately eleven o'clock and then went to bed?"

"Yes, around eleven."

"Then you were in your client's bedroom until approximately eleven o'clock?"

"Yes."

"You went in there following the termination of the conference to which you testified yesterday?"

"Yes."

"And remained there all during that time?"

"Yes."

"Are you certain you didn't leave the premises?"

"No, I . . ." his voice trailed away into silence.

"Go on," Mason said.

"I don't see that it makes any difference," Duncan snapped, flashing a swift glance at the district attorney.

Blaine jumped to his feet. "Your Honor," he said, "it's objected to as incompetent, irrelevant and immaterial, and not proper cross-examination."

"Overruled," Judge Markham snapped.

"Come to think of it," Duncan said, "I *did* go out for a few moments."

"Did Mr. Maddox accompany you?"

"Yes."

"Where did you go?"

"We went to a drug store a couple of blocks from the house."

"How long were you there?"

"About ten minutes."

"And during that ten-minute period, what did you do?"

"That's objected to as incompetent, irrelevant and immaterial and not proper cross-examination. The direct examination of this witness related to the fixing of time and to the time when he went to bed. The witness fixed that by testifying what he did during the evening. When the defense shows that the witness went out, it makes no difference where he went or what he did. It is only a question of determining how long he was gone."

"I think I'll sustain the objection," Judge Markham announced.

"Did you put in a telephone call?" Mason asked.

"Same objection."

"Same ruling," Judge Markham snapped.

"Isn't it true that at exactly eleven o'clock in the evening you were putting in a telephone call to Mrs. Doris Sully Kent in Santa Barbara, and therefore couldn't have been in the residence of Peter Kent?"

"Same objection," Burger snapped.

"If Counsel will amend that question so that witness is asked whether he wasn't putting in a long distance telephone call at some other place at the time when the witness has previously stated he had returned to the house, I will permit the question," Judge Markham ruled. "But I do not think it is necessarily relevant, pertinent or proper cross-examination to include in that question the name of the person to whom the telephone call was being made."

"Very well," Mason said, "didn't you put in a telephone call at exactly eleven o'clock from the drug store, Mr. Duncan?"

"It was before eleven. Five minutes to eleven. We were back in the house by eleven o'clock."

Mason smiled and said, "That's all."

Burger and Blaine held a whispered conversation, then Burger announced, "No further questions, Your Honor. Our next witness is Edna Hammer. I think the Court will realize that this young woman, who is a niece of the defendant, is a hostile witness. It may be necessary for me to interrogate her by leading questions. . . ."

"We'll cross that bridge when we come to it," Judge Markham interrupted. "Miss Hammer, take the stand."

Edna Hammer came forward, was sworn, and seated herself in the witness stand. Her face was pale and drawn. "Your name is Edna Hammer, you're a niece of the defendant, and you resided with him at his house at 3824 Lakeview Terrace, Hollywood?"

"Yes, sir."

"And were so residing there on the night of the thirteenth and the morning of the fourteenth of this month?"

"Yes, sir."

"Are you familiar with the appearance of a certain carving knife which was customarily kept in the top drawer of the sideboard in the defendant's residence?"

"Yes, sir."

"Did you see that knife on the morning of the thirteenth?"

She lowered her eyes, bit her lip and said nothing.

"Answer the question," Judge Markham ordered.

"I saw a knife which resembled it."

"Where was that knife?"

"Objected to as incompetent, irrelevant and immaterial," Mason said.

"We propose to show, Your Honor, that it was in the possession of the defendant," Burger stated.

"Upon that assumption, the objection is overruled."

"Answer the question," Burger said.

"*A* carving knife, similar in appearance to the one customarily kept in the sideboard drawer, was in my uncle's bedroom, under the pillow of his bed."

"That was on the morning of the thirteenth?"

"Yes."

"What did you do with the carving knife?"

"I replaced it in the sideboard drawer."

"Did you mention finding it to your uncle?"

"No."

"Did you take precautions of any sort to see that this carving knife did not come into the possession of your uncle after you had so replaced it in the sideboard drawer?"

"I locked the sideboard drawer on the evening of the thirteenth."

"And when did you next see the carving knife?"

"I don't know."

"You don't know?"

"I saw *a* carving knife, but I am not certain that it was the same one."

"I call your attention to the knife introduced as People's Exhibit Number Two. Did you see that knife on the morning of the fourteenth?"

"Yes. . . . I guess so."

"Where?"

"Under the pillow of the bed in Uncle's room."

"And it was in approximately the same condition that it now is? That is, with reference to the stains on the blade?"

"Yes."

"Now, then, when you locked that sideboard drawer on the evening of the thirteenth, was the knife inside the drawer?"

"I don't know."

"Why don't you know?"

"Because I didn't open the drawer to look."

"Who was with you at that time?"

"Objected to as incompetent, irrelevant and immaterial," Mason said.

"Overruled."

"Mr. Mason."

"You mean Perry Mason, the attorney, seated here in the courtroom?"

"Yes, sir."

"Is this knife, People's Exhibit Number Two, different in any way from the knife which you placed in the sideboard drawer on the morning of the thirteenth?"

"I don't think so. It is similar to the knife

which I put in the drawer there at that time."

"When you made a statement to the officers on the morning of the fourteenth you stated it *was* the same knife, didn't you?"

Judge Markham glanced over at Perry Mason as though expecting to hear an objection, but Mason remained motionless and attentive.

"Yes, I guess so."

"Now you will only admit that it's similar to the knife you found under your uncle's pillow on the morning of the fourteenth and placed in the drawer. Can you explain the apparent discrepancy in these two answers?"

"Only that when I came to think the matter over, I realized that many knives might look alike."

"And so far as you know, this knife, People's Exhibit Number Two, is the same knife which you found under the defendant's pillow on the morning of the thirteenth and placed in the sideboard drawer, is that right, Miss Hammer?"

"It is similar in appearance to that knife," she said.

"Cross-examine," Hamilton Burger announced triumphantly.

Mason began his questions soothingly. "How did you happen to discover the carving knife under your uncle's pillow on the morning of the thirteenth, Miss Hammer?"

"I . . . I . . . was worried about him."

"In other words you had reason to believe that he might have been walking in his sleep the night before, is that right?"

"Yes."

"And your anxiety about his sleepwalking was due to the fact that it was approaching a period of full moon?"

"Yes," she said in a low voice.

"How did you know, Miss Hammer, that sleepwalkers are more apt to become active during the full of the moon?"

"I read it."

"In a book?"

"Yes."

"A medical book?"

"Yes."

"Where did you get that book?"

"I sent away for it."

"You'd studied that book prior to the time you locked the sideboard drawer?"

"Yes, sir."

"Over how long a period of time?"

"Perhaps six weeks or two months."

"Now, directing your attention to this

knife, Defendant's Exhibit A, I will ask you if you have ever seen that knife before?"

"Yes, sir."

"Did you put that knife in the sideboard drawer at a date subsequent to the murder, in accordance with instructions from me?"

Hamilton Burger jumped to his feet, started to object, then slowly sat back in his chair.

"Yes, sir."

"I told you, I believe," Mason said, smiling over at the district attorney, "that I desired to plant that knife in the sideboard drawer and have it discovered the next day by Sergeant Holcomb; that I wanted to confuse the issues and make it increasingly difficult for the district attorney to get witnesses to identify the murder knife as the one which had been in the sideboard drawer, didn't I?"

District Attorney Burger blinked his eyes as though doubting his senses. Judge Markham leaned forward, started to say something, paused and stared at Mason, his eyes wide with astonishment.

Blaine jumped to his feet. "Your Honor, I think Counsel should be warned that, if this question is answered in the affirmative, the district attorney's office cannot afford to ignore the cold record, but will take steps to see that such unprofessional conduct is . . ." The district attorney grabbed his assistant by the coat, pulled him back to his chair.

"Answer the question, Edna," Mason said, paying no attention to Blaine's comment.

"Yes, sir."

"And this knife which I gave you is the one which I have had marked for identification as Defendant's Exhibit A?"

"Yes, sir, I think so."

Edna Hammer's voice was low and embarrassed. Her eyes reflected the confusion of her mind.

"And you did lock this knife, Defendant's Exhibit A, in the drawer?"

"Yes."

"But it wasn't there when you opened the drawer the next morning?"

"No, sir."

Mason said kindly, almost conversationally, "So you've known you were walking in your sleep for about six weeks or two months, Edna?"

The counsel at the district attorney's table were deeply engaged in a whispered consultation. The question slipped by their ears unnoticed. Edna Hammer, her mind in a half daze by the brazen manner in which Mason had publicly proclaimed their conspiracy, was thrown off her guard.

"Yes, sir," she said, mechanically.

It was Judge Markham who grasped the significance of the question and answer. He leaned forward to stare at the witness and said, "What was that answer?"

"Yes, sir," she said, and then suddenly realizing what she had said, "Oh, I didn't mean that . . . I didn't. . . ."

"What *did* you mean, Edna?" Mason asked.

"What's this? What's this?" Hamilton Burger shouted, getting to his feet. "I object. Not proper cross-examination."

"The question relating to her sleepwalking has already been asked and answered," Mason said. "I am now giving her opportunity to explain what she meant by her answer."

"And I object."

"Very well, Your Honor, I'll withdraw the question. The first answer speaks for itself," Mason said. Burger, looking very much annoyed, slowly sat down. Mason asked, in a kindly tone, "Did you habitually use that receptacle under the coffee table as a place in which to conceal articles from time to time, Edna?"

"Yes, sir."

"So that when you locked the sideboard drawer on the evening of the thirteenth and went to sleep with the thought uppermost in your mind that your uncle might get the carving knife in his possession while walking in *his* sleep, *you* walked in *your* sleep, and, not trusting the locking of the sideboard drawer to safeguard the knife, took the knife from the drawer and placed it in that oblong receptacle under the coffee table at exactly quarter past twelve, didn't you?"

"Objected to!" Burger shouted. "This is not proper cross-examination. This is argumentative. This is utterly improper. There is no proper foundation laid."

"Indeed there is," Mason assured the Court. "This witness has testified to locking the sideboard drawer; has testified to seeing the knife on the morning of the thirteenth, and to *next* seeing this knife on the morning of the fourteenth. I have the right to cross-examine her to show that she must have seen it earlier on the morning of the fourteenth, to wit, when she took it from the sideboard drawer."

"But," Burger protested, "if she did this while walking in her sleep, she wouldn't know anything about it."

"In that event," Mason answered, "she can answer the question by saying, 'I don't know.'"

Judge Markham nodded. "The objection is overruled," he said.

Edna Hammer said in a voice which was almost a wail, "I don't know."

Mason waved his hand in a gesture of dismissal. "That's all," he said. Hamilton Burger exchanged glances with young Blaine, then they plunged once more into whispered consultation.

"Any redirect examination?" Judge Markham asked.

"If we may have the indulgence of the Court for just a moment," Burger said, "this whole case has taken rather a peculiar turn." Blaine engaged in vehement whisperings but Burger slowly shook his head. Burger said, after a moment, "Very well, I'll ask Miss Hammer a few questions on redirect examination. Did I understand you to say that you had been walking in your sleep, Miss Hammer?"

"Yes."

"When did you first know that you were a sleepwalker?"

"About six weeks or two months ago. Perhaps a little longer."

"How did you find out you had been walking in your sleep?"

"I had been worrying about some rather important papers of Uncle Pete's. He'd left them in the writing desk in the living room. I told him I didn't think it was a safe place and he said it was all right, that no one would bother them. I went to sleep worrying about them and in the morning, when I got up, the papers were in my bedroom under my pillow."

Burger turned to Blaine. His manner was that of saying, "I told you so." Blaine squirmed uncomfortably, made more whispered suggestions to Burger. Burger whirled back to face her. "Why didn't you tell us this?" he asked.

"No one asked me."

"And you got this book on sleepwalking at that time?"

"I sent away for it, yes."

"Why?"

"Because I wanted to study up on it and see if I could cure myself, and I wanted to see if it was hereditary. In other words, I wanted to see if it might be a family taint."

"And did you do any more sleepwalking?"

"Yes."

Burger turned savagely to Blaine. Mason, looking across the gap between the counsel tables, grinned at the two lawyers who were carrying on a spirited argument in whispers, the hissing sibilants not sufficiently audible to allow spectators to hear what was being said, but loud enough to convey Burger's general tone of exasperation. "That's all," Burger snapped, overruling Blaine's whispered suggestions.

"Any recross-examination?" Judge Markham inquired of Perry Mason.

Mason shook his head. "No, Your Honor, *I'm* quite satisfied with the testimony of this witness as it is."

"That's all, Miss Hammer," Judge Markham said. "Call your next witness, Mr. Burger."

"Call Gerald Harris." Harris glanced solicitously at Edna Hammer as he came to the witness stand. She gave him a wan smile. When Harris had been sworn, Burger brushed aside a whispered suggestion from Blaine and began to question the witness. "Your name is Gerald Harris?"

"Yes."

"You are acquainted with Peter Kent, the defendant?"

"I am."

"You were in his house on the evening of the thirteenth?"

"I was."

"I show you a knife, Mr. Harris, which has been introduced in evidence as People's Exhibit Number Two, and ask you whether you have ever seen that knife before."

"I have, on several occasions."

"Where?"

"When I was a guest at Mr. Kent's house. That was the carving knife which Kent used to carve turkey and roasts. There was, I believe, a smaller carving set used for steaks."

"Do you know where this knife was kept?"

"I do."

"Where?"

"In the sideboard in the dining room."

"Do you know precisely where in the sideboard that knife was kept?"

"Yes, sir, in the top drawer. There was

a plush-lined section built to accommodate that carving knife."

"Did you have occasion to go to that drawer in the sideboard on the evening of the thirteenth of this month?"

"I did."

"At what time?"

"At approximately nine-forty."

"What were you doing?"

"Getting some accessories with which to make some drinks."

"Was the carving knife there at that time?"

"It was not."

"You're positive of that?"

"I am."

"Was there a lock on the drawer of that sideboard?"

"There was."

"Was that sideboard drawer locked or unlocked at the time you have mentioned?"

"Unlocked."

"Where were you at the time the crime was committed?"

"In Santa Barbara."

"Who sent you there?"

"Peter Kent."

"At whose suggestion?"

"At the suggestion of Perry Mason."

"Do you know whether Mr. Coulter, the butler, went to the sideboard drawer that evening?"

"I know of one occasion on which he went there, yes."

"Was that before or after the occasion on which you noticed the carving knife was not in the drawer?"

Harris fidgeted and said, "I would prefer not to answer that question."

"Never mind your preferences. You're here as a witness and under oath. Answer the question."

Harris said in a muffled undertone, "Before."

"Speak up," Burger said, "so the jury can hear you. What did you say?"

"I said that it was before."

"How do you know?"

"I saw Mr. Coulter at the sideboard."

"What was he doing?"

"He had the sideboard drawer open. I don't know whether he had been taking something out or putting something in. He closed the drawer and walked away."

"How long was that before you opened the drawer in the sideboard?"

"About five minutes, I would say."

Burger nodded triumphantly to Perry

Mason. "You," he said, "may cross-examine."

Mason inquired, almost casually, "By the way, you're secretly married to Edna Hammer, the witness who was just on the stand, aren't you?"

The courtroom, which had been tensely silent for some minutes, rustled with motion as the spectators leaned forward to catch Harris's answer. Harris hesitated a moment, then said, "Yes, I am."

"When were you married to her?"

"On the tenth of last month."

"Where?"

"In Yuma, Arizona."

"That marriage was kept a secret?"

"Yes, sir."

"Following that marriage Edna Hammer placed a spring lock on her bedroom door, did she not?

"Yes, sir."

"You," Mason asked, "had a key to that door?"

Harris showed his embarrassment. Burger jumped to his feet and said, "That, Your Honor, is objected to. It's improper cross-examination."

"I'll withdraw the question," Mason said, "subject to my right to ask it later, after

I have laid a proper foundation." Burger once more slowly sat down, his manner that of being ready to leap instantly to his feet. Mason, sprawled out in his chair with his long legs crossed in front of him, seemed to be enjoying himself immensely. "So you went to Santa Barbara on the night of the murder?" he asked.

"Yes, sir."

"And that was at my suggestion?"

"It was."

"Who went with you?"

"Miss Warrington, Mr. Kent's secretary."

"Anyone else?"

"No, sir."

"You're positive of that?"

"Yes, sir."

"You went, I believe, to the residence of Mrs. Doris Sully Kent?"

Burger said, "Just a moment, Your Honor, I think that question is plainly incompetent, irrelevant and immaterial and not proper cross-examination. It makes no difference where he went or what he did while he was in Santa Barbara."

Mason smiled and said, "Counsel, himself, has opened the door, Your Honor. In endeavoring to show the jury that I was in charge of things at the house and had sent this witness to Santa Barbara, he asked him where he was at the time of the murder. I, therefore, have the right to inquire most painstakingly and in the greatest detail in order to explore this phase of his testimony."

Judge Markham started to say something, then checked himself and said, "Objection overruled."

"Answer the question, Mr. Harris. Did you go to Mrs. Doris Sully Kent's residence?"

"I did."

"What did you do on arriving in Santa Barbara?"

"I went to Mrs. Kent's house. A Mr. Jackson from Mr. Mason's office was watching the house. He offered to stay on duty until two o'clock, but I knew he had work to do in court in the morning so I told him to take Miss Warrington to a hotel and I'd stay there to watch the house. He and Miss Warrington drove away in Mr. Jackson's car and I parked my car where I could see the house, and waited until I was relieved by a private detective some time around eight or nine o'clock in the morning."

"Were you there in front of Mrs.

Kent's residence at three o'clock in the morning?"

"Yes, sir."

"What happened?"

"Mrs. Kent received a telephone call."

"Could you hear what she said over the telephone?"

"Yes."

"What was it?"

"Your Honor," Hamilton Burger protested, "the vice of this entire line of questioning now becomes apparent. This witness is hostile to me, friendly to the Defense, as was plainly evidenced by his manner in answering the one important question for which I called him. Now, under the guise of cross-examination, and by the use of leading questions, the defendant is seeking to establish something which could not be established on direct examination."

"But, Your Honor," Mason pointed out, "Counselor himself asked this witness where he was at the time of the murder, and . . ."

"And you desire to test his recollection by cross-examination upon this particular point?"

"Yes, Your Honor."

"I think," Judge Markham said, "that the ruling of the Court will be that you may examine him as to where he went, what he did and what he saw, and generally what he heard, but not specifically as to what other persons may have said in his presence; I think that's going too far afield, particularly if it covers matters which may either be inadmissible, or may only be admissible as a part of the defendant's case."

"Very well, Your Honor."

There was a moment's silence. "Proceed, Counselor," Judge Markham said to Perry Mason.

"At the time that telephone conversation took place, where were you?" Mason asked.

"Across the street from Mrs. Doris Sally Kent's residence."

"Do you know her personally?"

"Yes."

"Did she answer the phone in person?"

"Objected to," Hamilton Burger. snapped, "on the same grounds. Counselor Mason can't prove his case by cross-examining my witness."

"I can if he opens the door on his direct examination," Mason insisted.

"I think I'll overrule that objection," Judge Markham said. "It might test the recollection and credibility of the witness. However, I'll not permit his recollection to be tested by a showing of what that conversation consisted of. I think that's a part of the defendant's case."

"Did she answer the telephone?" Mason asked.

"Yes."

"Did you see her clearly?"

"Yes."

Mason said, "By the way, did you know . . ." Mason stopped abruptly in midsentence, as, swinging about in his swivel chair, his eyes rested on the crowded courtroom. Suddenly he was on his feet. "Your Honor," he said, "I happen to notice that Mrs. Doris Sully Kent is in the courtroom. I understand that Mrs. Kent was originally subpoenaed by the Prosecution but, in view of the fact that certain legal proceedings had been instituted by her seeking to set aside a divorce decree, there is some question as to whether she is competent to testify as a witness *against* the defendant in this action. A short time ago a complete settlement of the various claims under dispute was negotiated, so that the final decree of divorce in the case of Doris Sully Kent versus Peter B. Kent has now dissolved the marriage between them. Inasmuch as Mrs. Kent is now in the courtroom, I wish to use her as a witness for the Defense. May I ask the Court to instruct Mrs. Kent not to leave the courtroom until I can have a subpoena served upon her?"

Judge Markham frowned, said, "Mrs. Doris Sully Kent, will you please stand up?" The blonde young woman arose while necks craned toward her. "You will not leave the courtroom," Judge Markham ordered, "until Counsel has an opportunity to serve s subpoena upon you, and in order to facilitate the immediate service of such a subpoena, the Court will take a recess of ten minutes, during which Mrs. Kent will be instructed not to leave the courtroom. During the recess the jury will remember the usual admonition of the Court not to discuss the case with anyone nor permit it to be discussed in your presence, and not to form or express any opinion as to the guilt or innocence of the accused until the case is finally submitted to you. Court will take a ten-minute recess."

Judge Markham started for his chambers. The courtroom became a babble of noise. Mason, stepping to the Clerk's desk, had the subpoena issued, handed it to the bailiff with instructions to serve it upon Mrs. Kent. Casually, Perry Mason strolled toward the door which led to the judge's chambers. He was joined by Hamilton Burger, who said, with frigid formality, "I think it would be well for us to visit Judge Markham together, Mr. Mason."

"Oh, very well," Mason assented. Together, the pair entered the judge's chambers. Judge Markham, seated behind a desk which was piled high with law books, looked up from the index of the Penal Code which he was reading. His manner was that of one who has been interrupted in a hasty search for something important.

"I didn't want to make the suggestion in front of the jury, Judge Markham," Burger said, with cold formality, "but I feel that Mr. Mason's conduct amounts to a contempt of Court."

"*My* conduct?" Mason asked.

"Yes."

"In doing what?"

"In deliberately planting that duplicate knife in the sideboard drawer in order to confuse the authorities in the case."

"But I didn't plant any knife with any such purpose," Mason said.

Judge Markham frowned, his face was

grave with concern. "I am afraid, Counselor . . ." he began. At something he saw in Mason's face he paused abruptly.

Burger said vehemently, "You can't get away with that, Mason. Edna Hammer has sworn absolutely, on her oath, that such were your intentions."

"But she doesn't know anything about my intentions," Mason pointed out. "She isn't a mind reader. She didn't qualify as a telepathic expert."

"But she testified that you told her what your intentions were."

"Oh, yes," Mason admitted, "I *told* her that."

"Am I to understand," Judge Markham asked, "that you now claim you made a false statement to her?"

"Why, certainly," Mason said, lighting a cigarette.

"What the devil are you getting at?" Burger inquired.

Mason said, "Oh, I knew she must have been walking in her sleep. You see, Burger, she had the only key to the sideboard drawer, and yet the knife had disappeared. Of course, there was some chance that Kent might have picked the lock or had a duplicate key, so while Kent was in jail, I thought I'd make another test. My theory was that Edna Hammer was herself a sleep-walker; that she was worried about her uncle, and went to bed with the thought of that carving knife preying on her mind. My experience with her, when she hid a cup in the receptacle under the coffee table, convinced me she had used that place to conceal things in before. So what more natural than that she should worry about the knife in her sleep, decide the sideboard drawer was not a safe hiding place, arise and, clad only in a nightgown, unlock the sideboard drawer, take out the knife, lock the drawer again and hide the knife in the receptacle under the table? I felt that the only way I could find out about this was by duplicating the circumstances, so I gave her another carving knife and impressed upon her how important it was that it should be locked in the drawer. It was a moonlight night and she went to sleep with the knife on her mind. Habit reasserted itself. When I start introducing *my* case, Mr. Burger, I shall show that this knife marked Defendant's Exhibit A was the same knife which I gave her to place in the sideboard drawer, and that it was subsequently discovered by one of Paul Drake's detectives in the oblong receptacle under the top of the coffee table."

"Do you mean you're going to claim *she* killed Rease?" Burger shouted. "Why, that's preposterous! It's absurd!"

Mason inspected the end of his cigarette. "No," he said, "I don't think I'll make any such claim. My case will doubtless be developed as we go along, Mr. Burger, but this discussion was confined to a suggestion on your part that I be considered in contempt of Court and also, I presume, held for disciplinary action on the part of the Bar Association. I merely mentioned this in order to explain that I had simply been conducting a test."

Mason turned and strolled from the chambers. Slowly Judge Markham closed the Penal Code, put it back into place in the row of books along one side of his desk. He looked at Burger's face and tried to keep from smiling. "I," the district attorney said, "will be damned." Turning, he stamped from the chambers.

Judge Markham, looking over the courtroom, said, "You have now served your subpoena, Mr. Mason?"

"I have."

"I believe Mr. Harris was being cross-examined?"

"Yes."

"Come forward, Mr. Harris."

There was no response. Burger, craning his neck, said, "Perhaps he has stepped out for a moment."

"I had one more question I wanted to ask on cross-examination of Mr. Maddox," Mason said, "we might fill in time by having Mr. Maddox come forward, if the Court will permit me to reopen the cross-examination for the purpose of asking that one question."

"Any objection?" Judge Markham asked of Hamilton Burger.

"I may say for the benefit of Counsel," Mason said, "that the question has become necessary because of unforeseen developments, to wit, the fact that Mrs. Doris Sully Kent is going to be a witness."

"No," the district attorney said, "I'll make no objection to having the witness recalled. I think I have a question that *I* would like to ask him on redirect examination."

"Mr. Maddox will please come forward," the bailiff said. Once more there was no answering stir from the witnesses in the courtroom.

"Have you some other witness you can call?" Judge Markham inquired.

"Begging the Court's pardon," Mason said, "I would like to finish with the cross-examination of Mr. Harris before the case goes any further. The only exception I think I would care to make would be to ask a single question of Mr. Maddox."

"Very well," Judge Markham said.

There were several seconds of uncomfortable silence, then Judge Markham whirled around in his chair. "The Court will take a brief recess, during which the bailiff will find the missing witnesses," he said.

Mason turned around to Peter Kent, slapped his hand down on Kent's knee, whispered, "All right, Peter. Within thirty minutes you'll walk out of this courtroom a free man."

—XXII—

MASON, ENTERING HIS office, scaled his hat at a marble bust of Blackstone. The hat struck squarely, spun half around, and slid over on the statue's head at a rakish angle. Della Street tried to be casual, but her eyes were starry. "Over the goal line, eh, Chief?"

"Right between the goal posts."

"When did you get wise?" she asked.

"Darned if I know," he told her, sitting on the edge of the desk and grinning boyishly, "Little facts kept pricking away at my consciousness. Why the devil should Edna Hammer have been reading up on sleepwalking? Why should she have put a lock on her door? Why did the figure that Duncan saw walk across the patio stop at the little coffee table; and why did the knife that was locked in the sideboard drawer disappear? Why did Maddox call Mrs. Kent at three o'clock in the morning, when he knew that a conference had already been arranged? I discounted most of Duncan's testimony because I figured he was just one of those egotistical ducks who would commit unconscious perjury. Give him a button and he'd sew a vest on it. But he'd undoubtedly seen *someone* walking around in a nightgown. When he said he put on his glasses he was a damn liar. He hadn't. All he'd seen was a white-robed figure walking around in the moonlight.

When he surmised, from subsequent events, that this figure must have been Kent, he hypnotized himself into believing he'd recognized Kent. He was sufficiently partisan to make himself more and more positive. But that didn't clear up the mysterious telephone conversation. Maddox was shrewd enough to avoid committing himself on the telephone call which Duncan put in around eleven o'clock in the evening to Mrs. Kent. His answers on direct examination didn't give me any inkling that he'd been present. I intended, of course, to cross-examine Duncan about any prior telephone calls, because Mrs. Kent's statement over the telephone that a conference had already been arranged through Maddox's lawyer indicated Duncan had been in touch with her. But Maddox did definitely state he hadn't telephoned Mrs. Kent at three o'clock in the morning. I didn't figure he'd perjure himself about something which could be checked up on. That made me start concentrating on Harris, and the minute I did that, I realized I was on the right trail. Harris was the one who had upset the apple cart all the way along the line. He'd been trying to get Kent convicted. When he realized Kent might have a good sleepwalking defense, he tried to blow it up by stating that the knife wasn't in the drawer when Edna locked it. He allowed himself to be subpoenaed as a witness. He'd evidently telephoned in an anonymous tip or two to the district attorney's office. Someone tipped Holcomb off that I'd been getting a duplicate knife to introduce to the case. When I asked Edna, she said she hadn't told anyone; but later on she must have told Harris."

"You weren't really trying to mix the knives up, were you, Chief?"

"Of course not. All I was trying to do was to impress on Edna's mind the importance of that knife in the sideboard drawer, so that she'd go to sleep with that thought uppermost in her mind."

"And then you figured she'd walk in her sleep again?"

"Yes."

"And take the knife?"

"Yes."

"And what did you think she'd do with it?"

"If my reasoning was right, she'd do the same thing she did before, of course—put it under the top of the coffee table. It was her little private hiding place for things she didn't want discovered."

"And Harris knew that?"

"Of course he knew it. He'd been surreptitiously living with her as her husband for over a month. He had a key to the house and a key to the new lock Edna had installed on her bedroom door. Moreover, the clews which pointed to him fairly screamed for attention. He'd been watching the house in Santa Barbara. If he'd been where he said he was, he'd have seen Mrs. Kent leave the house, get out her car and start for Los Angeles. He didn't see it. Therefore, he wasn't there. But, *if* he wasn't there, where was he? He could tell what she said over the wire. How could he have done that if he hadn't been there? There was only one other explanation: *He'd* been the one who had put in the telephone call. As soon as I considered that possibility, I realized that it was the only explanation. It had been right there in the open all through the case, clamoring for attention, and we simply hadn't thought of it. Harris, ostensibly, was watching the house in Santa Barbara to see that Mrs. Kent didn't leave. He wanted to rush back to Los Angeles, commit a murder, and then return to Santa

Barbara. He realized that if Mrs. Kent left the house in the meantime, it would be highly advisable for him to know that fact. Therefore, he decided to call her on the long distance telephone. Naturally, he couldn't use his own name. Looking around for a plausible name to use, he picked on Maddox, because he figured it was a logical development for Maddox to try to get together with Mrs. Kent. The trouble was it was *too* logical; too well thought out. Through Duncan, Maddox had already telephoned to Mrs. Kent. By that telephone conversation, Harris accomplished two results which were very valuable to him. First, he made certain that Mrs. Kent was at her residence at three o'clock in the morning; second, he took notes of everything that she said so he could repeat the conversation and thereby make it seem he was there in Santa Barbara within a few minutes of the time the murder was committed."

"But why did he want to murder Rease?"

"He had two reasons. Rease was the only other heir to Kent's fortune, aside from Edna Hammer, who had recently become Harris's legal wife. By murdering Rease, he got one heir out of the way and then, by pinning the crime on Kent, he was going to have the hangman get Kent out of the way."

"But Kent had made a will disinheriting Edna."

"No, he hadn't. He was going to make such a will after Harris married Edna. That was why Harris arranged to have the ceremony a secret one. He thought he'd have a chance to get Kent out of the way before Kent learned of the marriage and changed his will."

"But Harris himself was the one who asked Kent to change the will."

Mason laughed and said, "That was a mighty ingenious touch. Harris is an adventurer, an exploiter and an opportunist. He realized that Edna Hammer was a mighty attractive young woman who was going to inherit a considerable fortune. He also had looked up the situation enough to know that Kent was kicking out every suitor who might be a fortune hunter. So Harris beat Kent to it by asking him to disinherit Edna after he married her. He was playing the same game Pritchard was. He'd picked up a little stake from somewhere and was using it to give himself a swell front, hoping he'd be able to marry a wealthy woman."

"But what if Kent had taken him at his word and had already changed the will?"

"No," Mason said, "Kent was too much of a business man to do anything like that. He wanted to be certain Edna was happily married before he made a new will. Looking back on it, I don't think Harris planned murder from the start. You see, he was just a sheik with enough money to put up a good front, and an ambition to marry into some real coin. He started, I think, as an opportunist, just one step at a time. First he wanted to get legally married to Edna. Then he saw such a splendid opportunity to get both Rease and Kent out of the way that he couldn't resist it. Edna had told him about Peter's previous history of sleepwalking, then, when Harris realized that his wife was walking in *her* sleep, taking the carving knife from the sideboard and hiding it, then going back to bed and going to sleep, Harris conceived the idea of capitalizing upon Kent's sleepwalking propensities. Therefore, on the night of the twelfth, after Edna had pulled her sleepwalking stuff and gone back to a sound slumber, Harris took the knife from where she had secreted it, slipped quietly into Kent's bedroom, after first unlocking the door with the key he had taken from Edna's purse, and planted the knife under Kent's pillow. Kent found it in the morning and was paralyzed with fright. Edna also found it. Both of them jumped at the conclusion Kent was walking in his sleep again. Edna knew she was a sleepwalker, but didn't know she had been getting the knife from the sideboard. Therefore, she didn't suspect herself. Harris had everything planned for a murder. I don't know how *he'd* planned it, but when the Santa Barbara business came up he changed his plans so as to take advantage of it. Harris had set the stage. All he needed was to find a good alibi. I unwittingly played into his hands by giving him the chance to go to Santa Barbara, return to Hollywood, and slip into Kent's residence. He had the key which Edna had given him. He only needed to go to the coffee table in the patio and raise the lid. If the knife hadn't been there, he might have had some other scheme of murder. I don't know. But the knife *was* there. All he had to do was take it, kill Rease, go to Kent's bedroom— by this time he'd had a duplicate key made to Kent's door—slip the knife under Kent's pillow and start back for Santa Barbara."

"Then it couldn't have been three o'clock in the morning when Duncan saw the sleepwalker?" Della asked.

"Certainly not. It was quarter past twelve. That was where coincidence happened to play right into Harris's hands."

"He skipped out?" she asked.

"Sure. As soon as he heard me say that Mrs. Doris Sully Kent was in the Courtroom and we'd reached a compromise, he knew that she'd testify about that telephone conversation, and tell me frankly about the conference with Maddox and Duncan. Harris realized early in the game that the fact she had left for Los Angeles right after that telephone conversation was a circumstance which was going to put him on the spot, if anyone happened to appreciate the full significance of what must have happened. And Duncan's testimony about Maddox and he being together when they called Mrs. Kent at eleven o'clock damned Harris."

"And Maddox skipped out, too?"

"Yes. He was mixed up in that fraud so that *his* only hope of coming out on top of the heap was to get a good settlement from Kent. With Kent in jail, he hoped to deal with Mrs. Kent. When he saw that door was closed, he slipped. He wasn't running away from a murder charge, he was running away from a fraud charge."

"But would there have been a case against Mr. Kent if Rease hadn't changed bedrooms with Maddox?"

"Trace that back," Mason said, "and you'll find the suggestion came from Harris. Rease was a hypochondriac, and all Harris needed to do was to suggest he should change bedrooms in order to avoid a draft, and the thing was as good as done. Remember that Harris was the fair-haired boychild around that house. Likeable, magnetic and all of that, he enjoyed the confidence of everyone."

"Was the district attorney flabbergasted?" she asked.

"So damned flabbergasted he listened to me explaining the clews in the case to him in the Judge's chambers and stuck his cigar back in his mouth wrong end to, and burnt his mouth out of shape," Mason said, chuckling delightedly as he recalled the spectacle.